AMERICAN HUMORISTS SERIES

NEGRO MINSTRELS

Charles Townsend

LITERATURE HOUSE / GREGG PRESS
Upper Saddle River, N. J.

791.1
T 66 n

Republished in 1969 by
LITERATURE HOUSE
an imprint of The Gregg Press
121 Pleasant Avenue
Upper Saddle River, N. J. 07458

Standard Book Number—8398-1972-2
Library of Congress Card—70-91098

Printed in United States of America

THE AMERICAN HUMORISTS

Art Buchwald, Bob Hope, Red Skelton, S. J. Perelman, and their like may serve as reminders that the "cheerful irreverence" which W. D. Howells, two generations ago, noted as a dominant characteristic of the American people has not been smothered in the passage of time. In 1960 a prominent Russian literary journal called our comic books "an infectious disease." Both in Russia and at home, Mark Twain is still the best-loved American writer; and Mickey Mouse continues to be adored in areas as remote as the hinterland of Taiwan. But there was a time when the mirthmakers of the United States were a more important element in the gross national product of entertainment than they are today. In 1888, the British critic Grant Allen gravely informed the readers of the *Fortnightly*: "Embryo Mark Twains grow in Illinois on every bush, and the raw material of *Innocents Abroad* resounds nightly, like the voice of the derringer, through every saloon in Iowa and Montana." And a half-century earlier the English reviewers of our books of humor had confidently asserted them to be "the one distinctly original product of the American mind"—"an indigenous home growth." Scholars are today in agreement that humor was one of the first vital forces in making American literature an original entity rather than a colonial adjunct of European culture.

The American Humorists Series represents an effort to display both the intrinsic qualities of the national heritage of native prose humor and the course of its development. The books are facsimile reproductions of original editions hard to come by—some of them expensive collector's items. The series includes examples of the early infiltration of the autochthonous into the stream of jocosity and satire inherited from Europe but concentrates on representative products of the outstanding practitioners. Of these the earliest in point of time are the exemplars of the Yankee "Down East" school, which began to flourish in the 1830's— and, later, provided the cartoonist Thomas Nast with the idea for Uncle Sam, the national personality in striped pants. The series follows with the chief humorists who first used the Old Southwest as setting. They were the founders of the so-called frontier humor.

The remarkable burgeoning of the genre during the Civil War period is well illustrated in the books by David R. Locke, "Bill Arp," and others who accompanied Mark Twain on the way to fame in the jesters' bandwagon. There is a volume devoted to Abraham Lincoln as jokesmith and spinner of tall tales. The wits and satirists of the Gilded Age, the Gay Nineties, and the first years of the present century round out the sequence. Included also are several works which mark the rise of Negro humor, the sort that made the minstrel show the first original contribution of the United States to the world's show business.

The value of the series to library collections in the field of American literature is obvious. And since the subjects treated in these books, often with surprising realism, are intimately involved with the political and social scene, and the Civil War, and above all possess sectional characteristics, the series is also of immense value to the historian. Moreover, quite a few of the volumes carry illustrations by the ablest cartoonists of their day, a matter of interest to the student of the graphic arts. And, finally, it should not be overlooked that the specimens of Negro humor offer more tangible evidence of the fixed stereotyping of the Afro-American mentality than do the slave narratives or the abolitionist and sociological treatises.

The American Humorists Series shows clearly that a hundred years ago the jesters had pretty well settled upon the topics that their countrymen were going to laugh at in the future—from the Washington merry-go-round to the pranks of local hillbillies. And as for the tactics of provoking the laugh, these old masters long since have demonstrated the art of titillating the risibilities. There is at times mirth of the highbrow variety in their pages: neat repartee, literary parody, Attic salt, and devastating irony. High seriousness of purpose often underlies their fun, for many of them wrote with the conviction that a column of humor was more effective than a page of editorials in bringing about reform or combating entrenched prejudices. All of the time-honored devices of the lowbrow comedians also abound: not only the sober-faced exaggeration of the tall tale, outrageous punning, and grotesque spelling, but a boisterous Homeric joy in the rough-and-tumble. There may be more beneath the surface, however, for as one of their number, J. K. Bangs, once remarked, these old humorists developed "the exuberance of feeling and a resentment of restraint that have helped to make us the free and independent people that we are." The native humor is indubitably American, for it is infused with the customs, associations, convictions, and tastes of the American people.

PROFESSOR CLARENCE GOHDES
Duke University
Durham, North Carolina

January, 1969

The minstrel show, in which white male performers with cork-blackened faces impersonated Negroes, appeared in America early in the nineteenth century. About the turn of the century, Negroes shared comic roles with "stage" Irishmen and "stage" Yankees, but no attempt had been made to present "Negro life"—even in caricature—to the public. Minstrels first appeared in interludes between plays in the legitimate theater. These lively little sketches became increasingly popular and eventually provided an entire evening's entertainment.

An enterprising actor named Thomas Rice is credited with staging the first full-fledged minstrel show. Rice had been fairly successful as a blackface comedian. One day in 1828 in Cincinnati, he heard a black man or a street urchin—the accounts differ—singing this ditty:

Step first upon yo' heel
An' den upon yo' toe,
An' ebry time you turns around
You jump Jim Crow.
Next fall upon yo' knees
Then jump up and bow low
An' ebry time you turn around
You jump Jim Crow.

He jotted down the words, worked up a song-and-dance routine, and in the true American spirit of big-scale promotion, made a fortune in productions bearing savory titles such as *Jumbo Jim, The Virginia Mammy,* and *Bone Squash Diavolo.* The term "Jim Crow," which today means any sort of discrimination against black people, came out of Rice's shows. Rice himself played the role of "Jim Crow": a shuffling, obsequious Kentucky-cornfield Negro in Solon Robinson's play *The Rifle.* Rice played this part with great success in Louisville, Cincinnati, Philadelphia, New York, and London. In London the chimney sweeps and apprentices were quick to imitate Jim's limping dance.

"Christy's Minstrels," the most renowned of the early shows, was established in Buffalo in 1842. Edwin P. Christy used many of Stephen Foster's beautiful tunes, and his minstrels played to packed houses in England and America for a decade.

Henceforth, the minstrel show generally followed the pattern set by Christy. In the first part, a single row of "Negroes" (Haverly's "Burnt-Cork Brotherhood") was seated on chairs. The humor consisted of exchanges between the "interlocutor," a "straight man," and Tambo and Bones, the "end men." There were also mock lectures and sermons of the sort written by William Levison. The humor—for it certainly could not be called wit—was lowbrow and leaned heavily on puns, the most childish form of verbal amusement. It was not obscene, if we can judge from surviving collections.

The second act, the "olio," was a variety entertainment made up of banjo players, clog dancers, perhaps a watermelon man. According to an English reviewer, Jack Haverly's "American and European Mastodon Minstrels" sang comic Irish songs—pretty far from de ole plantation!

The show concluded with an "after-piece," another variety entertainment. It frequently played up the combination of simplicity and low cunning attributed to Negroes by the all-white audiences. (Negroes were prohibited from acting in or attending these shows.) The "after-piece" also parodied popular plays, operas, and important persons.

Innumerable minstrel troupes toured the United States and Europe from 1850 until the First War. Although the genre died out in the 'twenties, it continued to influence radio shows ("Amos 'n' Andy," Rochester in "The Jack Benny Show") and performers such as Al Jolson. Contemporary Negro writers and a few movie producers are trying to efface the image of the black man which minstrel shows impressed upon the minds of white Americans for almost a century: the "darky shuffle," the atrocious dialect, wide lips, gold teeth, etc.

The great historian of the drama, Arthur Hobson Quinn, thought that "The main strength of negro minstrelry lay in its musical and picturesque extravagance, and its significance as drama is slight. Had it been the result of negro initiative it would have been more important, but in its inception it was burlesque rather than sincere imitation. . . ." And *The American Negro Reference Book* comments: "On the positive side, however, the white blackface minstrels introduced to the American public the entertainment values inherent in Negro material—before Negroes themselves could appear on Jim Crow stages."

Upper Saddle River, N. J.   F. C. S.
May, 1969

NEGRO MINSTRELS

WITH

END MEN'S JOKES, GAGS, SPEECHES, Etc.

———

FULL INSTRUCTIONS FOR GETTING UP DARKY
ENTERTAINMENTS.

———

BY CHARLES TOWNSEND,

Author of "Private Theatricals," "Social Games at Cards," "Early Vows,"
"On Guard," "Wonderful Letter," "Breezy Call," "Deception," Etc.

CHICAGO:
T. S. DENISON, Publisher,
163 Randolph St.

PREFACE.

The growing popularity of amateur minstrel entertainments, and the consequent demand for a practical and modern work on the subject, have led to the preparation of this book.

The advice given in the following pages is practical, and not theoretical. I have endeavored to be concise, not verbose, and simple, not complex.

Among the conundrums and "gags" will be found some already popular hits, re-arranged. But aside from these the work is entirely original.

I trust that this book will clear away the many perplexities of the young minstrel, and enable him to prepare an entertainment which shall bring smiles from his audience, and mutual satisfaction to all concerned.

CHARLES TOWNSEND.

CONTENTS.

NEGRO MINSTRELS.

A REVIEW OF MINSTRELSY.

People like to laugh. Anything that helps us forget for a time, the vexation, trouble and sorrow of daily life is to be welcomed and encouraged.

Probably there is no form of entertainment capable of producing so much innocent fun as a good minstrel show, and certainly there is nothing more popular with all classes.

Negro minstrelsy is comparatively of modern origin. Previous to 1841 there were no organized companies, although performers would occasionally black up and "do a turn"—singing new songs and introducing quaint dances. Many of the songs became vastly popular. Among them were : "Back Side Albany on Lake Champlain," "Jim Crow"—which Rice sang as early as 1830—"Zip Coon," "Clar de Kitchen," "Coal Black Rose," "The Long Tail Blue," "The Blue Tail Fly" and "Roll de Cotton." These old songs were mostly refrains learned from the Southern darkies. The melody was always original and often striking. Many of the songs were forgotten long ago, but some of them like "Zip Coon" and "Jim Crow," seemed destined to live forever.

The first regular minstrel company was organized in 1841 by Dan Bryant, and appeared at the Chatham theater in New York. The company was called the "Virginia Serenaders," and met with immediate success. They played an engagement in Boston, returned to New York for a season and then went to Great Britain where they remained nearly a year. Barney Williams and Cool White were in this company, which had a very successful season in the British Isles.

The famous "Christy Minstrels" were organized at Buffalo in 1842, by E. P. Christy. After traveling about the country for several years they finally located in New York, where they remained from March 22, 1847, until July 13, 1854. During these seven years the company cleared the tidy sum of $161,873. E. P. Christy retired from business in 1854 and died May 21, 1862.

Other companies now sprang up in rapid succession, and negro minstrels became a popular "fad," both at home and abroad. Mr. Lincoln was especially fond of this class of entertainment and "by special command" Queen Victoria had the "Ethiopian Serenaders" appear before her on which occasion history says she actually smiled.

Minstrel entertainments at the outset were very crude, compared with those of to-day. In the olden time, a violin, banjo, the bones and tambourine made up the "orchestra," and the entertainment consisted solely of songs, dances and "gags." To-day the leading companies have the best and highest salaried vocalists, musicians, specialists, "stump speakers" and negro comedians, and the entertainments are models of refined fun.

Amateur minstrel companies can be organized with very little trouble, and are the means of much harmless amusement. In the following chapter will be found complete instructions for organizing, making up, dressing, and in fact everything necessary to arrange an entertainment.

ORGANIZING.

With two "end men"—one to play the bones and the other the tambourine—and a dignified "middle man," you have the nucleus of a minstrel company. These three characters should be good singers, and the end men of course, must be able to imitate the negro dialect. To complete the "circle" of the first part, a number of other characters—say six or eight, are necessary. They have nothing to do in the first part beyond answering occasional questions and joining in the chorus. In the second part they can come in for songs and dances, banjo work, stump speeches, and the usual farce.

The middle man generally acts as stage manager, arranges the music and usually takes part in the farce. He should use good English, be grave, dignified and courteous, making as strong a contrast as possible to the loud and noisy end men. His song in the first part should be a ballad, leaving the comic songs to the end men.

The First Part consists of jokes, gags, stories and songs. The performers sit in a half circle, with the bones and tambourine at each end, and the middle man in the center. Black dress coats and pants, white vests and the usual wigs should be worn. The first part closes with a *finalé*, a short, laughable scene, in which the whole company takes part.

End Men should carefully avoid everything approaching vulgarity, and no offensive personalities should be introduced. Avoid slang, and let politics and religion alone.

Stump Speeches are always very popular, if original in thought, and well delivered. This book contains a number of excellent examples. In delivering a stump speech, let your costume be as comical as possible. If you are tall, wear a tight fitting suit, which will make you appear taller yet. On the contrary, if you are short and stout, emphasize it by wearing very loose clothing. Some stump speakers come on in a ragged suit and damaged "plug" hat, carrying an old-fashioned valise and huge umbrella. A negro stump speech, being only a burlesque, admits of any peculiarities you may choose to introduce.

The Song and Dance. A neat song and dance is an attractive part of the programme, but it must be well rendered to be effective. A good voice and graceful movements are necessary, but intricate steps are not required. The costume should be neat and tasteful, but the style may be whatever your fancy dictates. Use very few gestures and dance with as little exertion as possible. Amateurs should not attempt to do a "straight" double song and dance, without the most careful and thorough practice, as the movements must all be in unison—something very difficult to accomplish. A grotesque double song and dance is easy and laughable—especially if one of the performers wears female costume. The "dance" is merely a series of jumps, kicks and breaks in time to the music—feats which any one can easily master.

Costumes. The regulation dress for the first part has already been described. The end men dress the same as the others, except that very high collars and comical wigs are usually worn. The costumes for the farces, stump speeches, etc., are easily found. Old clothes, ancient hats, venerable carpet bags and umbrellas, linen dusters, big shoes, and odds and ends of all sorts will come into play. In negro minstrels the female characters are always assumed by men, and the costumes should be in keeping with the character. Most of the farces described elsewhere in this book, contain accurate descriptions of the various costumes required; and when no descriptions are given, the ordinary everyday dress is worn.

Properties. The word "properties" in a theatrical sense means the articles required by the performers. For instance, chairs, tables, umbrellas, brooms, carpet bags, etc., are "properties." It is customary to appoint one member of the company "property man" whose duty it is to look after the various articles required, and see that they are on hand the night of the performance. This is a very important matter, and a good property man is one of the most valuable members of the company. Without his watchful care everything is liable to get at sixes and sevens, and the most laughable farce may fall flat if some necessary property is missing. No unusual nor expensive properties are required in a minstrel entertainment, and whatever is needed should be obtained early in the day, so that there will be no delay nor confusion after the curtain rises.

Making up is a term meaning to prepare the face for the stage. Burnt cork, cocoa butter, carmine and wigs are all that negro minstrels require. You can prepare the burnt cork yourself by obtaining a quantity of corks, placing them in a metal dish, pouring alcohol over them and burning them to a crisp. Powder and mix with enough water to make a rather thick paste. This trouble can be avoided by securing the prepared burnt cork, which may be had from any dealer in theatrical supplies, for a trifle. Carmine is a brilliant red powder which is used on the lips of the end men, to make them appear larger, and cocoa butter is an indispensable article for removing the burnt cork *without using soap or water*. The end men make up as follows: First rub a cake of cocoa butter lighlty over the face, ears and neck; then apply a broad streak of carmine to the lips, carrying it well beyond the corners of the mouth; then take a little of the prepared burnt cork, moisten it with water, and rub it carefully on the face, ears, neck and hands, being careful to avoid touching the lips. Put on the wig, wipe the palms of the hands clean, and the make up is completed. The other characters make up in exactly the same way, except that no carmine is used. For elderly negroes, like "Uncle Tom," wrinkles must first be drawn across the forehead and around the eyes, with India ink. The burnt cork is reduced with whiting to make it lighter, and is applied as usual, except that the lower eyelids and lips are covered with the regular shade of black, which will give them the sunken look of old age.

To Remove Burnt Cork.   Rub the features lightly with a cake of cocoa butter, and the burnt cork may be wiped off with a dry cloth.

Wigs.   All dealers in theatrical supplies furnish negro minstrel wigs at reasonable prices, and it is more economical to buy them than to manufacture them yourself.   However, if it is not convenient to purchase your wig, you can make a very fair substitute in the following manner: Secure a tight fitting, black skull cap, made of light but strong cloth, and cover it with curled hair, such as is used for filling mattresses.   For an end man's wig, the style may be as fantastic as you wish.   A female wig requires large puffs on each side, another at the back.   The gray curled hair is used for old negroes, and a large bald spot is left on the crown. A "fright" wig is quite effective at times, but if one is used it should always be purchased from a dealer, as no amateur wig maker can manufacture one properly.

Rehearsals.   All the business between the middle man and end men should be carefully rehearsed.   All must be "letter-perfect" in their lines, for if the proper questions and answers are not given, the gags will fall flat.   The *finalé*, which closes the first part, and the farce or farces in the second part also require careful and thorough rehearsals. Pay particular attention to the business of the piece, and don't hurry things.   The funniest point in many negro farces is the intense would be dignity of some of the characters.   Now if the scene is rushed through, all this is lost and the humor is not apparent.   Therefore in a scene of this sort, take plenty of time to elaborate the business.

The Performance.   There are a number of methods for opening the first part.   One is to have the performers all seated in their places and join in the opening chorus at the rise of the curtain. Then the middle man asks after the health of the end men, who return comic replies. A ballad usually follows, after which the end men get off a series of conundrums. Then one of them sings a comic song, after which the other end man gets off his gags. Another ballad, usually by the middle man, follows, and the first end man gives his gags, followed in turn by a comic song by the other end man. Thus each end man has a set of gags and a song. The remaining ballad is now given, after which the middle man announces the *finalé*. The curtain is lowered after the *finalé*, and when it rises again, the second part begins. This includes stump speeches, songs and dances, farces, etc.

On the next page is a sample programme, which will serve as an excellent guide to the amateur in preparing a progamme for the evening.

As every enterprise depends largely on proper advertising, I would suggest that your programme be printed in full on your circulars to be distributed around town. People are more disposed to attend a show when they know just what they will get. Many companies fail in this particular. *Judicious* advertising always pays. If you have a few large posters with "scare" heads, placed in advance, give only general outlines on them and refer to "small bills." This will cause people to read the small bills when distributed.

The Big Four Minstrels.

PROGRAMME.

Bones, *MR. SMITH.*   Middleman, *MR. JONES.*   Tambo., *MR. BROWN*
Stage Manager,   -   -   -   -   -   *MR. JONES*

PART I. ALL SORTS.

OPENING CHORUS, - - -		BIG FOUR MINSTRELS
BALLAD, -	"*The Song of the Steeple,*" -	MR. KELLY
COMIC SONG, -	"*No Use Waitin',*" - -	MR. SMITH
SOLO AND CHORUS,	"*Dreamy Eyes,*" - -	MR. JONES
COMIC SONG, -	"*Swim de Golden Ribber,*"	MR. BROWN
SONG AND CHORUS,	"*Climb Up, Chillun,*" -	MR. JENKINS
GRAND FINALÉ, -	"*Rapid Transit,*"	BIG FOUR MINSTRELS

PART II. GRAND OLIO.

MR. JAMES SMITH,
The Wizard of the Banjo, in Songs, Solos and Sayings.

MR. H. R. BALDWIN,
The Song and Dance-Artist, in his famous Specialties.

INTERLUDE: "ALL EXPENSES."
ARTEMUS BUZ, a Theatrical Manager, - - MR. JONES
JEMIUS FLUTICUS, a hard up "Coon," - MR. BROWN

MR. THOMAS KELLY,
The Modern Cicero, in his Famous Oration, "Natural Nature."

The whole to conclude with the Roaring Farce entitled
THE DARK TRAGEDIAN.
JUNIUS BOOTH SNUFFLES, who wants to Act, - MR. SMITH
MOSE GETSUM, who wants the Earth, - MR. JENKINS
PETER SNOOZE, who wants to Sleep, - - MR. BROWN

DOORS OPEN AT 7.30.   .   .   .   .   CURTAIN RISES AT 8.
ADMISSION, 25 CENTS.

CONUNDRUMS.

Throughout this work it will be observed that the middle man is always addressed as "Mr. Johnsing," the end man who plays the bones as "Mose," and the tambourine player as "Sam."

Why is a fat man always rich?
Because he is never poor.

What kind of a face does a beggar prefer?
One that is for-giving.

And what kind does an auctioneer prefer?
One that is for-bidding.

Why is a good base ball player like a spider?
Because he catches flies.

What has three feet, yet never walks?
A yard.

When is a long man short?
When you ask for the loan of a dollar.

When does a pig become real estate?
When he is turned into a field.

What kind of a box has neither weight nor shape?
A box on the ear.

Why do old maids have no equals?
Because they are matchless.

What article of food is the rarest?
Butter made from the cream of a joke.

Why do you find a bar-room like a bad dollar?
Because you can't pass it.

What kind of a lock is hard to pick?
A lock of hair from a bald head.

When does a woman hold her jaw?
When she has the toothache.

Why do you always keep your word?
Because no one will take it.

What is it that nobody touches, yet often breaks?
Silence.

What is nothing?
A sleeveless coat without a body.

When does a farmer resemble a dentist?
When he is digging out stumps.

What is the difference between a brave soldier and a modern belle?
One faces the powder, and the other powders the face.

Why is grease like a sewing society?
Because it makes (s)candles.

Why are soldiers tired out on the first of April?
Because they have just finished 31 days of March.

Why is a cock fight always fair?
Because there is no foul play.

Why cannot whiskey be conquered?
Because the more you down it the quicker it downs you.

What musical instrument resembles a poor hotel?
A violin (vile inn).

Why is a piece of flannel like a tramp?
Because it shrinks from washing.

What is the best way to stop a chimney from smoking?
Put out the fire.

What pain can never be cured?
A pain in the head of navigation.

What word does your wife like best?
The last one.

When is a ship in mid ocean not on the water?
When she's on fire.

Why is a dog's tail like the heart of a tree?
Because it is farthest from the bark.

What smells most in a refinery?
The nose.

How can you learn the value of money?
Try to borrow some.

Why is your nose in the middle of your face?
Because it's the scenter.

Why is life an unanswerable conundrum?
Because we all give it up.

What is the latest in dresses?
Night dresses.

When is a girl not a girl?
When she is a little sulky.

When is a bed not a bed?
When it is a little buggy.

What goes most againt a farmer's grain?
A mowing machine.

Why are women like facts?
They are stubborn things.

Why are hens very generous?
Because for every grain they give a peck.

Why did the boy stand on the burning deck?
Because it was too hot to sit down.

What was the longest day in Adam's life?
The day when there was no Eve.

GAGS.

These gags and stories must be carefully rehearsed, and delivered in an easy, natural manner. All should evince a lively interest in the questions, but extravagant gestures or any grotesque business must be avoided.

A WONDERFUL ESCAPE.

MIDDLE MAN. Well, Mose, you look worried.

BONES. I is worried.

MIDDLE MAN. What has disturbed your mental equipoise ?

BONES. Hey ?

SAM. Dat's just it—hay. Like all donkeys he eat too *much.*

BONES. I scorn de base collusion.

MIDDLE MAN. Well, what is the matter?

BONES. Ise finken' ob how I narrowly 'scaped losin' my life on the 'scursion yesterday. The steamer was full an' so was everybody else. De blue waves rippled an' de sunlight danced. De little birds filled de air wiv melody, an' de men filled demselves wiv beer. When all was bright, an' gay, an' happy an' nobody was finkin' ob de afterward hereafter, suddenly dere came an awfully awful 'splosion, blowin' de steamer sky high an' killin' every man, woman, an' chile aboard de boat. Not a single soul was saved, not eben a keg of beer.

MIDDLE MAN. And how did you escape?

BONES. How did *I* escape ? I staid to home, dat's how.

TAMBO'S TROUBLE.

MIDDLE. Sam, I want to ask you a question.

TAM. All right Mr. Johnsing, extenuate yo' inquiry.

MID. What was the matter with you yesterday ?

TAM. Nuffin.

MID. Oh yes, there was. You seemed to be in a free fight.

TAM. Now I recomember. It was this way : Dat morning I rose, from my sweet repose, put on my clothes, down street I goes, met one o' my foes, his name was Mose, he was morose, I belicose, I trod on his toes, on pur*pose*, an' smashed his nose, as I suppose; he struck out blows, which as you knows I couldn't oppose; dey hits my nose an' down I goes, and de blood flows, into de gutter it goes, whar de water flows, den up I rose, an' brushed my clothes, an' home I goes, to my sweet repose, to dream o' my foes an' dat's all I knows.

BONES. Oh dos, de dos, de dos !

SOMETHING ABOUT SNAKES.

BONES. Oh Mr. Johnsing!

MID. What is it, Mose ?

BONES. Did you eber see a snake?

TAM. Did he ? Why his boots ah full uv 'em.

MID. I have seen snakes now and then.

BONES. Any big ones ?

MID. Yes.

BONES. How big ?

MID. Some were larger than the small ones, and the small ones were smaller than the large ones.

BONES. I see. Well, yo' jest orter see de snakes down aroun' our house. Such whoppers!

TAM. What an awful warnin' ginst drinkin' Indiana whiskey !

MID. You kill the snakes, I suppose.

BONES. Kill 'em ? *Kill 'em ?* Not much. Dem ar snakes am worth their weight in diamonds.

MID. In what way ?

BONES. Every way. I'll tole yo' erbout 'em. One day my little boy was settin' on de do' step, eating pie. 'Long came a funny little snake, an' my boy gin him a piece ob de pie. Yo' know snakes am berry fond o' pie. Well, dat snake eat de pie, an' den he laffed an' licked his chops, an' purred like er cat. Den my boy war workin' on his rifumtick lesson, an' dat ar snake clum up on his shoulders an' worked ebbery sum fo' him. He does all my book keepin' fo' me now. He kin run up a column o' figgers, ten feet long in two seconds, without a mistake.

MID. Wonderful.

BONES. Yes sah.

MID. What kind of a snake is it?

BONES. It's an adder.

MID. Is that all?

BONES. Oh no. Dar's a big black snake wot's very fond o' terbacker. I keeps a pipe fo' him, an' he comes in an' has a sociable smoke ebery night. Dat snake knows a pile. He gits under folkses winders an' squalls like a cat, an' den people fires fuel and shoes, an' bootjacks at him, and he brings 'em all home. Haint paid nuffin in ten years fo' wood, nor coal, nor shoes. But I most lost him once.

MID. How was that?

BONES. It war this way. He wont 'low no udder brack snakes 'round dar. He's mo'n forty feet long, and one day he looked outer de winder an' seed his own tail on de do' step. He frot it war anudder snake an' he chased dat tail 'roun' de house half a day. Arter a while he catched hold ob de tail, an' had just erbout swallered hisself when I kim in an' argified him inter lettin' up.

COLD WEATHER.

MIDDLE. I saw in the paper to-day that they are having very cold weather out west.

TAM. How cold?

MID. Thirty below zero.

TAM. You call dat cold?

MID. I certainly do. And I think, Sam, that you never saw any colder.

TAM Dar's whar you's way off, Mr. Johnsing. I went way up norf once, to discover de norf pole. Talk erbout cold. Why, de cattle's horns uster lop right down on dere faces, an' de fires friz, an' de best alcohol turned inter solid ice. An' ebery mornin' 'fore we ventured out, we uster stick a big crowbar out frew a hole in de roof.

MID. Why was that?

TAM. 'Cos ef de end war friz off we know'd it war too cold to go out.

SUDDEN CHANGES.

MIDDLE. When I arose the other morning, the air was soft and balmy; but in less than an hour the thermometer had fallen thirty degrees

BONES. Huh! Dat's nuffin. One day I was plowin' down in Texas. It was powerful hot, the frowmomater bein' a hundred an' twenty down cellar. One ob de mules drapped dead from sunstroke. Afore I got him onhitched de wedder changed so sudden dat de udder mule friz solid, an' fell dead standin' up! The frowmomater fell to sixty below zero an' biling water friz solid on er red hot stove.

A QUESTION.

MIDDLE. Sam, why is dancing like new milk?

TAM. Because it is good for the calves.

MID. In other words, do you mean to say that exercise of a terpsichorial nature benefits the understanding?

TAM. No I don't. But I do say dat if dancin' am good fo' de calf you orter try it.

MID. You're a *cow*ard to talk that way.

TAM. Am dat de *cream* ob yo' remarks?

BONES. He's got *butter* little mo' to say.

TAM. Oh, *chalk* it down!

BONES. *Cheese* it.

———

ABOUT THE LAW.

BONES. Oh, Mr. Johnsing.

MID. What is it, Mose?

BONES. Yo' understan' law, I is told.

MID. Yes, I have studied law for many years.

BONES. Pr'aps de law 'lows yo' ter know enuff ter tole me dis. Kin a man be indicted as bein' a *loose* character, wheu he comes home *tight* every night?

———

QUITE CORRECT.

TAM. Mose, does yo' know dat Mr. Johnsing allers drinks perpen'diculer?

MID. Perpendicular, what do you mean?

TAM. Why sah, yo' takes yo' whiskey *straight*, isn't dat perpen'dicler?

———

IGNORANCE.

BONES. Sam, yo's jest de ignorantest culled pusson I ebber seed.

TAM. I knows jest as much as yo' do, any day.

BONES. Get out! Yo' haven't as many brains as a hog.

MID. Here, this won't do. We can have no quarreling here.

BONES. I don't car'. He *haint* got es many.

MID. How do you make that out?

BONES. Easy enough. He has only his head full, while a hog has a whole hogshead full.

THE BAKERY.

MIDDLE. Mose, I heard you apply an unusual epithet to a yellow darkey recently.

BONES. Did it hurt him?

MID. I don't know, but if you had applied the same name to me I would have punched your head! The idea of calling a man a cake.

BONES. A cake?

MID. Yes, a cake.

BONES. Nuffin bad 'bout dat. He was a cake. We's all cakes.

MID. What kind are we?

BONES. Black cake.

MID. What kind of a cake is a prize fighter?

BONES. He's a pound cake.

MID. And what would you call a lawyer?

BONES. He's a sponge cake.

MID. What is a pretty girl?

BONES. Oh—she's a sweet cake.

MID. And an old man?

BONES. He's a frosty cake.

MID. Well—what would you call Sam?

BONES. He's a hard—seed cake.

MID. What is an old bachelor?

BONES. He's a stale cake.

MID. And an old maid?

BONES. She's tart cake, made without sugar.

A HEALTHY REGION.

MIDDLE. Sam, I heard you had purchased a plantation in Alabama.

TAM. Dat's jes what I'se done. Cost me $40,000.

MID. All paid for, I hope.

TAM. Co'se it am. Paid $11 down, an' gib my note fo'
de balance. Dat's de way I does business.

MID. Is it a healthy locality ?

TAM. Healthy ? Well I should snicker to snort.
Healthy ? Why nobody eber dies on dat plantation—not
even de niggers—dey jes dries up and blows away. Dar
hasn't been a docter dar sence Christofo Columbine 'scov-
ered Chicago.

MID. It must be a great sanitarium.

TAM. A which unarium ?

MID. A sanitarium—a place where sick people go to re-
cover their health.

TAM. Zactly. Last summer a sick man kim dar from
de Norf. He war awful sick. He had de confused, con-
founded consumption ob de liver. His lungs war all gone
an' he breaved frew his gills like a fish. He brought his
coffin an' pall bearers along, an' had his habituary notice
all made out, an' a doctor's certificate ob def in his pocket.

MID. Well ?

TAM. Well ? I should say well. He kim to my plantation, an' yo' nebber seed a man improve so. 'Fore he'd
been dar an hour he turned a hand spring, kicked de bottom
outer de coffin, licked all de pall bearers, sassed my mudder-in-law, chased a nigger ten miles wivout stoppin', drank
a gallon ob tangle foot, made a temp'rance speech, jined de
church, cut an' piled ten cords o' wood, an' gained forty-
seven pounds in weight.

MID. Is that so ?

TAM. Co'se it am. Den he sent fo' his wife, an' when
she got dar she was awful sickly. Had fever an' ager, chills,
malaria, lumbago, plumbago, pneumonia, old-monia, non
compus mentis, rheumatism, corns, bunions, earache, liver
complaint, mumps, measels, twins and poor health. She
was so poor dat she uster go an' lean up agin a sunbeam an'

she couldn't hardly lift up her voice, nor hold her bref without droppin' it. Fore she'd been dar an hour she spanked de twins, run my mudder-in-law outer de house, mose killed a sassy tramp, did four weeks washin', milked twenty cows, churned a hunnerd pounds of butter, an' killed a hen wiv a rock.

BONES. Say—did she frow de rock?

TAM. Co'se she did

BONES. Dat settles it.

TAM. Settles what?

BONES. Your reppetation. I believed ebberyting up to dat rock story, but no livin' woman kin hit er hen wiv er rock, so I knows you's lyin'. Next.

NINE IN ONE

BONES. Oh, Mr. Johnsing.

MID. What is it, Mose?

BONES. Has yo' heard de sayin' dat a tailor is only de ninth part ob a man?

MID. Yes, I have heard the saying.

BONES. It's dead wrong—dead wrong. A tailor is nine men combined in one.

MID How do you make that out?

BONES. I'll remonstrate. *First* as a *capitalist*, because he *invests*. *Second* as a *gard'ner*, he *sews*. *Third* as a *sailor*, he often *shears* off. *Fourth* as a *lawyer*, he often *presses a suit*. *Fifth*, as a *wood dealer* he *axes* you what you'll have, and den cuts it out. *Sixth*, as a *sheriff*, he provides suspenders or *gallowses* for people. *Seventh*, as a *farmer* he *sews* an, *binds* an' *gathers*. *Eighth*, as a *cook*, he generally has a war·n *goose*, and *ninth*, as a *policeman*, he does a great deal of *sponging*.

MID. That's pretty good—eh, Sam?

TAM. It's so-so.

BONES. He don't catch the *thread* of it.

TAM. Dat's quite *needles.*

MID. You mean *need-less.*

BONES. You should not *tuck* him up like dat.

TAM. I might have *fell* down ef he hadn't.

MID. Oh, *bind* up your tongue. One would think you a Wheeler & Wilson sewing machine.

BONES. He certainly is not *Domestic.*

TAM. Well *Howe's* dat ?

MID. No matter, Mose, let's hear if you're a *Singer.*

A HURRICANE.

TAM. I say, Mr. Johnsing.

MID. Say it, Sam.

TAM. Dar was a termenjus storm down our way las' night—a reg'’ar harrycane.

MID. You mean a hurricane.

TAM Co'se I duz. De harrycane came, an' it blewed an' it blowed everything high low jack an' de game. Everything blowed down not stood up 'ceptin' my house.

MID. How did your house escape ?

TAM. Oh, it was mortgaged so heavy it couldn't stir.

OFF AND ON.

BONES. Yo' wears pow'ful good clothes, Mr. Johnsing.

MID. Yes, Mose, a gentleman should always be well dressed.

BONES. Dat's me. I change my suit sebben times ebbery week.

MID. Seven times ? Then you must have at least seven suits.

BONES. No, I'se only got one.

MID. Then how do you make seven changes every week ?

BONES. Why—I changes it off at night an' on in de morning.

A NARROW ESCAPE.

TAM. I seed a most horrible awfui blood freezin' sight las' night.

MID. Where was it, Sam?

TAM. Down at de depot. You know dat de nine o'clock train comes in about eight sixty P. M.

ALL. Yes, yes. Go on.

TAM. An' yo' know she comes in wiv a fizz, an' a sizz, an' a whizz.

ALL. Yes, yes!

TAM. Don't get excited.

ALL (*excitedly*). Of course not—of course not. Go on! Go on!

TAM. Well dar was a pore ole blind man what couldn't see nuffin kase he were blind. An' he war standin' right dar on de track as de nine o'clock train kim in at eight sixty.

ALL. Well, well! Go on!

TAM. An' de train was comin' like sixty, and de crowd yell like sixty too. An' dar stood dat pore ole blind man what couldn't see, right on the track when de nine o'clock train kim in at eight sixty.

MID. So you said.

TAM. Co'se I did. An' de crowd yelled, "Get outer de way!" an' de bungineer blowed his bell an' rung de whistle an' de train kim bileing an' fizzin' an' sizzin' an' whizzin' right to'rds dat pore ole blind man who stood right dar on de track kase he couldn't see nuffin jes as the nine o'clock train—

MID. But, man alive, then what?

TAM. Den what? Why (*carelessly*) de train stopped, an' de blind man went home.

FACTS AND FANCY.

MIDDLE.   Mose, do you know the difference between fact and fancy ?

BONES.   I does.

MID.   Can you give us an illustration?

BONES.   Suttenly.   It am a *fac'* dat yo' owe me five dollars, Mr. Johnsing, an' I *fancy* dat it'll be a frigid day in August when I gets de money.

TAM.   I'll lucydate de difference 'tween fac' an' fancy.

MID.   Give it to us.

TAM.   I fancy dat I'll ask dis crowd to take a drink.

ALL. (*eagerly*).   All right.

TAM (*turning away*).   But de fac' am I wont.

ALL (*sit disgustedly*).   Oh !

A QUESTION OF FAITH.

MIDDLE.   I was reading the other day a very interesting article which opened to my mind—

BONES.   What did yo' use—a can opener ?

TAM.   How *can* you do it ?

MID.   No sir, I did not use a can opener.   The subject was faith.   Now Mose, do you know what faith is ?

BONES.   Co'se I does.   Faith am a compounded conglomeration ob phantasmagorical whichness, absolved from someness by a liberal infusion ob de impossibly mixed up when.

MID.   What in creation are you talking about ?

BONES.   I dunno.

MID.   I was speaking of faith, which evidently you fail to comprehend.   Now I'll explain.   Faith is the evidence of things unseen—or in other words, believing what you have not witnessed.   To illustrate: You believe what I say.

BONES.   Not when you talk politics.

MID. I'll make it clear. I tell you for instance, that I saw a sky-blue dog climb a tree backward. You did not see it, but you believe my word. That is faith.

BONES. Oh—I see.

MID. Now do you know what faith is?

BONES. I does.

MID. Then suppose you tell these gentlemen.

BONES. Faith is—is a *sky blue dog backin' up a tree.*

SIGNS OF THE TIMES.

TAM. Mose, I seed a queer sign in a store to-day.

BONES. What was it, Sam?

TAM. De sign said: "Wanted—women to sell on commission."

BONES. Huh! Dat's nuffin. I saw'd a sign in a corset store what read: "All sorts of ladies' *stays* here."

TAM. Ob *corsets* a *steel*, so don't *spring* any more like dat on us, or I'll *whale* yo' *bones.*

SCIENCE AND ART.

BONES. Oh, Mr. Johnsing.

MID. Well, Mose?

BONES. Kin yo' expostulate de difference 'tween science an' art?

MID. I can explain—certainly. Science is knowing how to do a thing, and art is doing it.

BONES. Berry good. But dar's one fing what science don't know how to do, an' which art can't do.

MID. What is that?

BONES. Make Sam's mouf any bigger wivout movin' his ears.

TAM. Fink yo's smart. But I know one fing dat art can't do.

BONES. What am dat?

TAM. Make a ripe watermellin safe in yo' hands.

MODEST.

TAM. Mose, is yo' a good speller?

BONES. Yes sah. Is you?

TAM. Pretty consid'ble good.

BONES. What does m-i-l-k spell mostly?

TAM. It mostly spells water.

BONES. What does c-h-a-i-r spell?

TAM. You's got me now, Mose.

BONES. Yo' don't know? Why, what's yo' sittin' on?

TAM. (*bashfully*). Oh pshaw! I won't tell. So now.

THE CREAM OF THE JOKE.

BONES. Seems to me, Sam, dat de milk we gits now'days am pow'ful weak

TAM. I hab noticed dat dar's no cream on it.

BONES. Can yo' splain de cause?

TAM. I can. Yo' see the price has riz, an' milk is now so high dat de cream can't reach de top.

BONES. Oh, cheese it.

THE GIRLS.

TAM. Mose, does yo' know why old maids prefer de capital ob Ireland?

BONES. Suttenly. Case dey all want *Dublin*.

TAM. My gal is drefful absent minded. Las' night she kissed de candle an' blowed me outer doors.

BONES. My gal am pow'ful modest. She allers goes inter her dressin' room when she wants ter *change her mind*.

TAM. My gal wont peel pertaters.

BONES. Why not?

TAM. Cos dey's got eyes an' might git mashed on her

IN BUSINESS.

TAM. Mr. Johnsing, I hear dat you's gone inter de milk business.

MID. That's quite true, and I am very successful.

TAM. I jedge so. I saw yo' buyin' a lot er chalk dis mo'nin'.

MID. That's to *chalk* down your account, for you never pay.

TAM. Well who would pay fo' ole skim milk?

MID. I do not skim my milk.

TAM. Yes yo' do. Yo' skims it on top an' den yo' turns it ober an' skims it on de bottom.

MID. I hear that you have opened a jewelry store.

TAM. Am dat so? When, when was it?

MID. Last night, with a crowbar.

FISH IN VARIETY.

BONES. I say, Mr. Johnsing, did yo' ebber fink dat fish am like folkses?

MID. I don't know that I ever did.

BONES. Well sah, dey am, fo' a fac'.

MID. Can you give us a few illustrations?

BONES. Wiv de mos' excrutiatin' pleasure.

MID. Well, then, what is a rich man?

BONES. He's a *gold* fish.

MID. Very good. And what would you call a fat man?

BONES. He's a *whale*.

MID. What would you call a great actor?

BONES. He's a *star* fish.

MID. What is a dude?

BONES. A dude is a *weak* fish.

MID. What is a lawyer?

BONES. A lawyer am a *shark*.

MID. What is my little boy?
BONES. He's a *sun* fish.
MID. What is a mean, selfish, ugly man?
BONES. A *dog* fish, ebbery time.
MID. And what is Sam?
BONES. A big *cat* fish, more mouf dan brains.
MID. And what would you call me?
BONES. You? You's'a rum-*sucker*.

TWO AND ONE.

TAM. I has a queernundrum fo' yo' Mr. Johnsing.
MID. Go ahead, Sam.
TAM. A man bought two fish an' when he got home found he had three fish. Does yo' ketch on?
MID. No. I fail to see the point. How was it?
TAM. He had two fish—an' one smelt.

TAMBO'S WIFE.

MIDDLE. Yon have been a widower for some time, Sam.
TAM. Yes sah. Dat's er fac'.
MID. Do you ever intend to marry again?
TAM. I'se 'fraid not sah. De fac' o' de matter is I'se 'fraid I nebber kin fine anudder wife like my first one—so car'ful—so savin'.
MID. She was a good manager, then?
TAM. Manager? Why, Mr. Johnsing, dat ar woman had no equal in dat line. She'd take one o' my ole coats an' outer dat coat she'd make a superfluous suit o' clothes fo' bofe my boys, besides a cap an' a pair ob slippers fo' me, an' outer de linings she'd construct enuff towels an' napkins an' pocket handkerchers to las' us a year. She'd make a pair o' winder curtains outer an ole sock an' a splendiferous rag carpet outer a pair ob my ole trouserloons. An' bake!

Her biscuits was so light we nebber used lamps, an' she'd make lovely pineapple dumplings' outer pine chips. She nebber wasted nuffin. She'd make booful chicken fritters outer six cent beef, an' she'd cook potato parin's so you'd fink dey was canvas back duck. She'd make ox-tail soup outer de tail ob a coat, an' fry up pine shavin's so you'd swar dey was Saratoga chips. Manage? Well, I reckon.

A GREAT NEED.

BONES. Mr. Johnsing, why are men like dough?
MID. Because they are apt to rise.
Bones. No sah.
MID. Then because some are light, and some are heavy.
BONES. No *sah*.
MID. Then why *are* men like dough?
BONES. Because de women (k)need 'em.

ASTRONOMY.

MIDDLE. Mose, did you ever study astronomy?
BONES. Yes sah. I'se studied my gal, who is a regular Venus.
MID. Then perhaps you know why the moon is called "she?"
BONES. Bekase she has a sun, who comes rolling home in de mornin'.
MID. You cannot blame him, when his mother gets full.
TAM. An' stays out all night.
BONES. Dat's whar her money goes. She often has only a quarter.
MID. Why are a girl's thoughts like the moon?
TAM. Kase dar's a man in it.

THE ——— !

TAM. Oh, Mr. Johnsing.

MID. Well, Sam, what agitates you ?

TAM. If de debble should lose his tail whar'd he gitter nudder?

MID. Where would he get another? Why, in a cheap saloon of course.

TAM. An' why so sah ?

MID. Because in cheap saloons they *retail bad spirits.*

BONES. Speakin' ob de ole boy, I has one fo' yo' Mr. Johnsing.

MID. Name it, Mose.

BONES. Why am de debble like a pawnbroker ?

MID. Because you go to both when you are hard up.

TAM. An' den dey's got him fast.

BONES. How you make dat out, yo' brack rascal ?

TAM. Co'se de debble an' de pawnbroker bofe claim de unredeemed.

_____

THE DIFFERENCE.

BONES. Mr. Johnsing, kin yo' tell de difference 'tween a man's wants an' a woman's wants ?

MID. I'm afraid not. Can you ?

BONES. Sartin. A man wants all he kin git.

MID. And a woman ?

BONES. A woman wants all she can't get.

_____

A TERRIBLE SIGHT.

TAM. I saw'd a terrible drefful awful sight on my way home.

MID. You alarm me, Sam. What was it ?

TAM. Oh, it was scrumptiously awful.

MID. Yes, yes. Tell us about it !

TAM. It was frightful. It made my ha'r bile an' my blood stan' on end.

MID. Come, come. Give us the facts.

TAM. Well sah, I seed a young man an' a young woman standin' on a gate bitin' each udder.

HOW HE FELT.

MID. I hear, Mose, that you got pounded by some loafers the other night.

BONES. Yes sah, I did, an' it made me feel like Lazarus.

MID. How was that ?

BONES. Why Lazarus was licked by de dogs, an' so was I.

LOST HIS SITUATION.

MIDDLE. You don't seem to be working these days, Sam.

TAM. No sah, I'se libin' on de interest ob my debts.

MID. You should not idle away the golden moments. Remember that an hour lost can never be regained.

TAM. Well, I had a job, but I resigned.

MID. Why so ?

TAM. Fo' a number ob reasons. De boss was a proud, haughty man, who had pie twice a day an' changed his socks ebbery month. He wanted me to be at work by nine o'clock in de mornin' an' he 'jected ef I took more dan two hours fo' my dinner. He didn't want me to smoke cigarettes durin' business hours, an, he wanted me to stop readin' de mornin' paper ef a customer kim in. He didn't want me to frow peanut shucks nor water mellun rinds on de flo' an' he 'fused to raise my wages. Finally he said he didn't want me no mo' no how, so I got disgusted an' quit.

ABOUT A BILL.

MIDDLE. Mose, I have some news for you.

BONES. Am dat so ? What am de nature ob de infliction ?

MID.   As I was strolling down the street this morning, I met a very handsome young lady who asked about you. Wanted to know if you were in jail.

BONES.   An' what did yo' say ?

MID.   I told her your time was up and you was out.

BONES.   An' what did she say ?

MID.   She said that as you was *out* perhaps you would step *in* and pay that little bill you owe her for board.

BONES.   Settle de bill ?

MID.   Yes sir, settle the bill.

BONES.   She better settle her coffee.

MID.   But she says the bill has been running a long time.

BONES.   Den let it walk awhile.

MID.   But you owe her, and you ought to pay.   She cannot afford to run a boarding house if people don't pay her.

BONES.   She can't ?

MID.   No sir, she can't.

BONES.   Den she better sell out to some one who can.

NEVER SAW IT.

TAM.   I know suffin you nebber saw, Mr. Johnsing.

MID.   What is that ?

TAM.   You nebber saw a big sized, small, white blackbird sittin' on a wooden stone on a moonlight day, eatin' a yaller blackberry.

BONES.   Keno!

CURIOSITIES.

MIDDLE.   Gentlemen, we were speaking recently of curiosities.   What is the greatest curiosity in the world ?

BONES.   A woman who can hit a hen wiv er stone.

TAM.   A girl who wont look in a mirror when she hab a chance.

MID.   An honest politician.

BONES. A this year's woman in a last year's bonnet.

TAM. A dude who has sense.

BONES. A man who nebber lies to his wife.

TAM. Dem am all great curiousities, but I hab a collection ob greater ones down at my house.

MID. Have you indeed ? What are they ?

TAM. A hunk ob cheese from de milk ob human kindness. A shavin' from de Board ob Aldermen. Some flint from de rock of ages. A walkin' stick made from a hurricane. Butter from de cream ob a joke. A bedstead from de Chamber ob Commerce. A feather from de tail ob a coat. Some shingles from de roof ob a mouth. A glove from de hand ob adversity. Teeth from de mouth ob a ribber. Some hair from de head ob navigation. A shoe from de foot of a hill. A suit ob clothes worn by de man in de moon. An egg laid by de tailor's goose; and a pillow from de bed ob a ribber.

HOW HE DID IT.

BONES. You's fond ob good libbin' I b'lieve, Mr. Johnsing.

MID. Yes, Mose, I *am* fond of good living.

BONES. You eats quail on toast, biled watermelluns, stewed cucumbers, nightengales tongues, champagne an' isters an' all de udder delicacies, I s'pose.

MID. Well I hardly go as steep as that.

BONES. Nor me. I confines myself ter pie.

MID. Pie ?

TAM. Yo' bet. He's berry pious.

BONES. I took a couple ob my frien's to a restaurant tudder day. We each called fo' a pie. De man only had one, yet we each had a pie.

MID. You did ?

BONES. We did.

MID. Do you mean to tell me that there was only one pie in the restaurant, and that the three of you each had one ?

BONES. Dat's what I said.

MID. Nonsense! I tell you it's impossible. How could he give you three pies when he only had one ?

BONES. He went out an' bought a couple.

FOWL TALK.

MIDDLE. I was astonished and grieved beyond measure, Sam, at the way you addressed a gentleman yesterday

TAM. Did I 'dress him wiv a brick-bat ?

MID. No sir, but you applied an opprobrious epithet.

TAM. Fo' de lo'd's sake! Wha's dat ?

MID. You called him an "antique dodo."

TAM. Correct.

MID. No it isn't correct. A "dodo" was a bird, or a fowl.

TAM. Well, we's all birds or fowls, as I can extenuate.

MID. Proceed.

TAM. Don't we all hab ter *scratch* aroun' to git a livin', an' don't we *crow* éf we do anyfing smart ? Don't old maids *cackle*, an' aint we all *laying* fo' a fat job ? Aint Mose a *black* bird, an' aint you a *goose* ? Aint——

MID. Hold on now!

TAM. Aint a nice young girl a dear little *duck*, an' aint my mudder-in-law an ole *hen* ? Don't yo' know lots of *chippies* an'——

MID. No I don't. But say, what would you call a prize fighter ?

TAM. He's a *sparrer*. (sparrow)

MID. Pretty good. What would you call a gambler ?

TAM. He's a *hawk*.

MID. And a green countryman ?

TAM. A *jay* bird.

MID. And a lawyer?

TAM. He's a *robin* everybody.

MID. What is a baby?

TAM. A *yeller* bird.

MID. And a man who is dead broke?

TAM. A *blue* bird.

MID. Any more?

TAM. Yes sah. Some men *swallow* a good deal an' some are fond ob *larks*. Some men *crow* too much, you often go on a *bat*, an' Mose am a reg'lar *nightingale*.

MID. In that case, Mose, perhaps you had better sing (*announces song*).

HOW IT HAPPENED.

MIDDLE. Mose, I observed that sometime ago you vanished from our view, and we saw nothing of you for six months or more.

BONES. Your prognostifications am lucid. I had a job.

MID. Doing what?

BONES. Gittin' my board fo' my clothes.

MID. I fail to comprehend.

BONES. Den I'll explasturate. Yo' see I had a little fallin' out wiv de sheriff ob New York, an' I concluded dat my health required a change. So I started fo' Philadelphia. An' as I had invested all my ready cash in government bonds, I concluded to walk. Arter I'd gone several miles I ran across a man who had tied his hoss to de fence an' was layin' asleep under a tree. I was sorter tired walkin' an' I spected de gemman was tired ridin', so I axed him would he let me take his hoss. An' what yo' fink he said?

MID. I'm sure I don't know.

BONES. Nuffin—jest nuffin. An' yo' know as "silence gibs consent," I onhitched de hoss an' rode off.

MID. You did very wrong sir.

BONES. Did I, well ef I'd a left de hoss dar, some tramp might a stole him.

MID. And I should say *you* stole him.

BONES. Don't you call me no thief, Mr. Johnsing.

MID. Well, go on.

BONES. I *did* go on. Arter a while I got ter finkin' dat pr'aps I *had* done wrong to take de hoss, seein' as how he warn't ezactly mine.

MID. So the pangs of conscience began to rankle in your breast?

BONES. Yes sah. An' de pangs ob de saddle 'gan to rankle me too. So I 'cluded dat it was wrong to take de hoss, an' wronger to keep him—an' den I sold him.

MID. That was very, very wrong. How much did you get for him?

BONES. I got—six months.

TAKEN FIRST.

TAM. Mr. Johnsing, kin yo' tell me what am taken 'fore yo' git it

MID. Anything you can get your paws on.

TAM. Ha! Ha! He mocks me. Master ob de bones, dost thou know?

BONES. I dust. Yo' photograph is tooken afore yo' git it.

THE RUNAWAY.

TAM. Oh, Mr. Johnsing.

MID. Explain your grief, Sam.

TAM. I had a heap o' trouble yes'day.

MID. In what respect?

TAM. I took my wife Hannah, an' my darter Dinah out fo' a drive. All went serene fo' a time, but bimeby we arrove at a bridge across a creek. Den de hoss she stopped an' wouldn't go an' Hannah took de lines, an' I took de whip an' began to larrup her—

MID. Larrup whom—Hannah?

TAM. No sah—de hoss. Den she yelled to stop or she'd run away.

MID. Who yelled—the horse?

TAM. *No* sah—Hannah. An' with that she histed up her heels an' kicked—

BONES. Who – Hannah?

TAM. *No* sah. You fool nigger. De hoss she kicked, an' she said I was er blamed fool—

BONES. Dat hoss had hoss sense.

TAM. Hannah said dat.

BONES. Oh!

TAM. Den she snorted an' rared up on her hind feet an'—

MID. Who snorted—Hannah?

TAM. No *sah*. De hoss, I tole yo'. An' she frowed her arms aroun' my neck an'—

MID. The horse?

TAM. Jerusalem! No—Hannah. Den she got de lines aroun' her legs an'—

MID. Why did Hannah do that?

TAM. Snakes an' grasshoppers! *It was de hoss!* An' den she laid her head on my buzzum an' wept—

MID. The horse wept?

TAM. Blunderbuses and rifled cannon! *Hannah wept!* At las' I got de lines an' mos' yanked her blamed head off an'—

MID. Shame on you to yank your wife's head off.

TAM. Ise—talkin'——erbout—de—hoss. Understand? De hoss. See? I yanked de hoss, an' de hoss got yanked by me.

BONES. A hoss on you. Well?

TAM. I pass. You seem to know more about it den I do. Next.

___

GUESS THE WEIGHT.

BONES. I killed a hog yesterday, Mr. Johnsing, and' what does yo' reckon he weighed ?

MID. Well, perhaps it weighed—

BONES. Now be car'ful. 'Member it was a big one.

MID. At a venture I will say it weighed—

BONES. Don't be rash, sah—don't be rash.

MID. If you will allow me to speak, I should say that it might have weighed 200 pounds.

BONES. Does you indeed ? I was talkin' about a *hog*.

MID. Well, say 300 pounds.

BONES. I said I killed a *hog*. It wasn't a *rabbit*. You guess.

A MAN. Four hundred pounds.

BONES. You's a pow'ful weak guesser. Has nobody got onter de idea dat I spoke ob killin' a *hog* ? You guess.

A MAN. Seventy-five pounds.

BONES. You's a fool. Sam, yo' guess.

TAM. Whose hog was it ?

BONES. Mine sah.

TAM. Who owned it ?

BONES. I owned it. It was mine. It belonged to me.

TAM. It weighed twice as much as half.

MID. To save argument, Mose, I will guess 500 pounds.

BONES. Gemmen, Ise talkin' erbout a *hog* dat I killed.

MID. Well then, 600—700—800—a *thousand* pounds.

BONES. Gemmen, once more let me relate de fac' dat I killed a *hog*.

MID. I guessed 1,000 pounds. Now for goodness' sake Mose, how much did it weigh ?

BONES (*carelessly*). I dunno. I didn't weigh it.

BEST OF ALL.

TAM. What am de best ob all de musical instruments?

MID. The violin.

TAM. Come off de bridge.

BONES. De bass drum.

TAM. You can't beat dat inter me. No sah. Pianos am de best ob all de musical instruments.

MID. Why so?

TAM. Co'se dey's upright, grand an' square.

WHITEWASHING.

MIDDLE. Sam, you seemed rather excited when you came in this evening. What had disturbed your equanimity?

TAM. My equa–what–ity?

MID. Equanimity—or in other words, your mental balance.

TAM. I see. Well you see I saw a row. It was between a black whitewasher an' a white whitewasher. De white whitewasher had tooken a job to whitewash a fence wiv whitewash. De black whitewasher axed de white white-washer fo' a job ter help whitewash de fence. So de white whitewasher tole de black whitewasher to go ahead an' white-wash while he sat down in de shade an' bossed de job. But de black whitewasher did not whitewash fas' enough to suit de white whitewasher, who said he was no good. Den de black whitewasher got sassy an' de white whitewasher blacked de eye ob de black whitewasher, whereupon de black white-washer banged de white whitewasher ober de head wiv his whitewash brush. De nex' minute de white whitewasher ketched de black white washer by de slack ob de pants an' soused him head first inter de bar'l o' whitewash an' when de black whitewasher came out he was as white as de white whitewasher. Jes den a cop arove on de scene, an' arrested bofe ob de whitewashers.

CONUNDRUMS.

BONES.   Mr. Johnsing, how is yo' on conundrums?

MID.   Very good, indeed.

TAM.   Ise glad you's good fo' suffin'.

BONES.   Here's one fo' you.   Why am a colt like a rich man's son?

MID.   Because he is apt to be frisky.

BONES.   Dat's correct, but not right.

TAM.   Because he feels his oats.

BONES.   No sah.

MID.   Because he's well heeled.

BONES.   Wrong some more.

MID.   Well, Mose, why *is* a colt like a rich man's son?

BONES.   Kase it wont do no work 'till its broke.

TAM.   Here's one fo' you, Mose.

BONES.   Lucidate yo' problem.

TAM.   Why am a stutterin' man unreliable?

BONES.   I gibs dat up.

TAM.   Kase he -nebber speaks wivout breakin' his word.

THE ANTHEM.

TAM.   Mr. Johnsing, did yo' ebber ha'r an anthem?

MID.   Frequently.

BONES.   What's an anthem?

TAM.   Fo' de enlightenment ob dat Africanius ignoramius I will proceed to liquidate.   Ef I say, " Mose, get me a banjo ' dat am *not* an anthem.   *But* ef I say "Mose, Mose, Mose, get, get, get, Mose get me, me, me, dat ban ban, me dat ban, jo, jo, jo, Mose get get, me me dat, ban ban jo, Mose—get—me—dat—ban—n—n -jo, Yawmen."   Dat's an anthem.

WHAT'S IN A NAME.

BONES. Mr. Johnsing, does yo' know Annie?

MID. Annie?

BONES. She's a berry lively gal.

MID. Annie who?

BONES. Annie—mation.

TAM. Mose, does yo' know Sal?

BONES. Sal?

TAM. She's a nice gal, an' yo' ought ter get her.

BONES. Sal who?

TAM. Sal—vation.

BONES. Mr. Johnsing, yo' fell down stairs yes'day.

MID. I did, from the top to the bottom.

BONES. Yo' must hev been hurt, as I heerd yo' call fo' Helen.

MID. I did not call for Helen.

BONES. Yes yo' did.

MID. I did not.

BONES. Yes yo' did—I heerd yo'.

MID. Call for Helen? Helen who?

BONES. Helen Blazes.

ALL. Oh, Mr. Johnsing!

FINALES.

After the Conundrums, Songs and Gags have been given, the middle man announces the *finalé.* All retain their places, except the principals, until the close.

RAPID TRANSIT.

AIR:—"Johnny comes marching home."

MID. (*sings*).

There was a man once on a time.

ALL.

There was, there was !

MID.

Who lived in a fever and ague clime.

ALL.

He did, he did.

MID.

He was a regular tough old clam,

He lived on hominy, hash and ham,

For people he didn't care a—(*all clap hands*).

ALL (*quickly*).

Johnny, fill up the bowl.

MIDDLE. Mose, did you ever think how much we owe to science ?

BONES. What sort er signs does yo' mean ?

MID. I said *science* not *signs*. For instance, the great discoveries such as the steam engine, the telegraph, the sewing machine, and the telephone.

BONES. Dat reminds me. Ise made an invention.

MID. What is it ?

TAM. A new way to work a free lunch route.

BONES. My invention sah, am a lightning transmitter by de means ob which yo' kin send anyfing yo' please by telephone.

TAM. Send me a house an' lot.

MID. Do you mean to say that you can transport anything you please by telephone ?

BONES. I does.

MID. I cannot believe it.

BONES. Den I'll prove it. Yo' call up somebody. (*Picks up a tin can fastened to a string running off the stage*). Sing out and I'll have him here in a jiffy.

MID. Well call up my brother.

BONES (*calls into can*), Hello, central ! Hello, Hell-o ! Say—connect me wiv de Bottomless Pit.

MID. Confound you! My brother is alive, and in New York.

BONES. All right (*calls*). Hello central! Hello, hello! Say—connect me wiv de New York jail.

MID. My brother is not in jail, sir.

BONES. All right (*calls*). Hello central! Hello! Say central, connect me wiv de brewery.

MID. My brother is not in a brewery. He is at number 4139 Broadway, New York.

BONES. All right (*calls*). Connect me wiv 4139 Broadway, New York. Hello, yes. Is dat yo' Mr. Johnsing? Yes. Yo' brudder is har an' wants to send yo' a message. What's dat? Send yo' de money he owes yo'—yes, he's out now. Only got six months. Hey? Oh yes 'bout de same puts on a clean collar once a month. (*To middle man*). Yo' brudder is axin' arter yo'. (*Calls*). What's dat? No sah. I keep my chickuns locked up.

MID. What *are* you talking about?

BONES. Yo' brudder is axin' arter yo'—dat's all. Would you like ter see him?

MID. Certainly I would.

BONES. Den I'll bring him (*calls*). Oh, Mr. Johnsing— would yo' mind comin' out har by telephone? All right. He's started. Jes' left New York. Now he's in Albany. Now he's in Syracuse. Now he's in Buffalo. What's dat? Oh yes. He stopped a few seconds in Buffalo fo' a drink. All right. He's started again. Now he's in Cleveland— buzz, buzz, don' yo' har him comin'? Now he's passin' Toledo. Dar! Whoo! Los' one ob his shoes! Chuck! Dar goes his hat! Now he's passin' frew Indiana—now he's getting nearer an' nearer, he's comin', he comin'—hey, look out! Ki! Yi! Biff! Bang! Whoop! (*Drops can. A man rushes in, flings* BONES *aside, climbs over the others and finally rushes up to* MIDDLEMAN, *shaking his hand as the curtain falls.*

NOTE.—The above description of the "journey" by tele-

phone can be varied to suit any locality. "Bones" must
work himself up, at the close, as if greatly excited, and the
others show mixed alarm and surprise. It will add greatly
to the effect if a "thunder sheet" is rattled, or a bass drum
struck occasionally during the description.

THE GREAT HITTERS.

AIR:—"Oh Dem Golden Slippers."

MID. (*sings*).

Oh my boxing gloves I have laid away,
And I'll slug no more till my dying day,
For the man that fights gets jugged, you know,
And his head is swelled in the morning.

CHORUS.

Oh, dem slugging sluggers,
Oh, dem slugging sluggers,
Allers git dere noses punched when dey chance to meet;
Oh, dem slugging sluggers,
Oh, dem slugging sluggers,
Slugging sluggers bound to slug den dey don't look neat.

BONES. Who was de strongest man ?

TAM. John L. Samson.

MID. Who first taught the noble art of self defense ?

BONES. De ant.

MID. The ant ?

BONES. Yes sah, de ant. Don't de good book say: "Go
to de ant thou slugger"—an' what would a slugger go to
de ant fo' 'cept to slug ?

TAM. Oh, what a fool niggar.

BONES. Don't talk like dat ter me, er I'll chuck yo' in
de mug.

TAM. Git out chile. I'd brush yo' aside like a cobweb.

BONES. Oh mamma ! Why you poor fool niggar, I kin tie yo' inter a bow knot an' stuff yo' inter a rat hole.

TAM. Yo' make me smile. Meet me by moonlight alone an' I'll mash yo' so flat dey could use yo' fo' a door mat.

BONES. Let me introduce yo' to dis foot, an' I'll kick yo' so high yo' wont get down afore Christmas.

TAM (*rising*). I'll mash yo' jaw.

BONES (*rising*). Come on yo' orang ertang.

MID. Come, come, gentlemen, this wont do. (*They sit*).

BONES. I'll lick yo' outer sight fo' two cents.

TAM. Bet yo' a thousan' dollars I kin knock yo' out in one round.

BONES. Put up de stuff.

TAM (*to* MIDDLE MAN). Loan me ten cents to bet him.

BONES. Put up now or shut up.

TAM. I kin shut yo' up.

BONES. No yo' can't.

TAM. Yo' anudder.

BONES. Go dar yo' self.

MID. Gentlemen, this unseemly quarreling wont do at all. If you are determined to meet in the fistic arena, you had better do so at once, and in a quiet, orderly way. I have gloves handy in my room, and if you agree to spar according to Hoyle, I will see fair play.

BONES. Dat's me.

TAM. Me too.

MID. Then prepare for the fray. (BONES *and* TAM. *exit*). Now, Isaac, if you will bring in the gloves, we will have this great question settled in short order. The gloves are in my room.

A MAN. All right, Mr. Johnsing. (*exit and quickly returns with two pairs of old boxing gloves covered with flour*).

MID. Meanwhile, gentlemen, I wish to impress you with the solemnity of the occasion. The gage of battle has been thrown down, and we are to judge this fight on its merits, to cheer the victor and be merciful to the vanquished. Let us therefore put aside all personal feelings, Let us judge not as Republicans nor Democrats nor Prohibitionists, but as the great and impartial public. And I caution you above all things to restrain your emotion, and indulge in no bets, nor loud words or the police may burst in upon us, and then, figuratively speaking, we will all be in the soup. Here come the champions. Get your places.

BONES *and* TAMBO *enter in extravagant ring costumes. They put on gloves, the others having drawn back their chairs, stand in half circle.* BONES *and* TAMBO *shake hands as* MIDDLE MAN *calls "time."* BONES *holds* TAMBO'S *hand and slaps his face with the other hand. Then follows a burlesque boxing match ad. lib. They fall down without being hit. They blow each other over. They embrace, each one hitting himself with his own gloves. They separate and strike wildly when at opposite sides of the stage. The* MIDDLE MAN *calls "Time" frequently and the crowd yells, cheers and bets. When the uproar is at its height, some one yells "Police!" and all rush frantically for the door, as the curtain descends.*

CURTAIN.

NOTE:—The burlesque boxing match is very funny, always eliciting roars of laughter, if well done. But it should be carefully rehearsed, so that the interest will not flag, and the various situations must be decided on in advance.

STUMP SPEECHES.

UNCERTAINTIES OF LIFE.

Fellow people an' Udder Folkses: · By de pressin' invitation ob de President ob de United States, de Queen ob England, de Cigar ob Russia an' de Jack ob Trumps, I hab concluded to honor you by dis oration.

Your dense ignorance am so great dat I must spoke berry plain, an' to de point. So I'll jes' say a word—dat is a few words—mo' or less—accordin' somewhat er how-mostly, mo' over, howsomebber, notwithstandin'.

Life am onsartin. Darfore took car' what yo' do, an' don't do nuffin ef yo' wife am industrious.

Nebber fool wiv guns what aint been loaded. I once knowed a niggah who looked down inter de dark an' silent insides ob an ole shot gun what hadn't been loaded since Adam was a boy; an' de nex' minute he went crashin' up among de stars, an' I spect he's up dar now. Anyhow, all we eber found ob him, was a toe nail an' de spot whar he had been.

Nebber use karsene ile to light de fiah. I had a yaller gal once to cook fo' me, an' she was pow'ful car'less dat way. One day I missed her. I also missed my house. She started a fiah wiv karsene ile, to cook a goose. She succeeded. She cooked my goose, an' her own goose too, an' de house wasn't insured.

Does yo' unnerstan' de whichness ob de if, de whyness ob de when, or de whereness ob de what? I reckon not.

Such bein' de case, let me negotiate yo' to avoid de
equinox ob a mule's hind heels. Nuffin but a nigger's head
am a match fo' de mule's heel, so white folks take warning,
an' be willing ter die some udder way.

Who among yo' ebber stop to reflect dat what we am to-
day, an' may be to-morrer, an' year arter nex' befo' las' am
not so much what we hencely hope in ruministical retro-
spection, as which we subsequently am or—or—sorter, so
to speak to de point.

Did you ebber stop to reflect how much we may ascertain
by findin' out ?

While yo' journey erlong life's tortured pafway, did yo'
ebber stop to ponder on de terrifyin' fac' dat de older yo'
grow, de longer yo' lib, an' darfore yo' orter flee from dat
which am what ?

Remember, moreover somewhat, dar what yo's do not
do now immegitly to once, or sometime in de future, ef
nobody else does it, will more or less remain undone forebber.

De sun could not sot ef he did not rose, an' de moon allers
has twenty-five cents—or a quarter—afore she gets full.

Dis am true not only ob all fings, but ob ebberyfing else.

On dis life de onsartin subsequently proceeds closely upon
de already mostly forgotten previously; an' de dark an' hazy
past was once de silent germ ob de twilight future, whar de
great unknown wrapped itself in de mantle ob de wide an'
boundless ultimatum henceforthly.

I often sometimes fink dat in my youthful young child-
hood ef I had not done exactly as I did, de chances is dat
I would hab done differently somewhat or more.

My deluded hearers, let me demolish yo' ter powder wiv
dese pow'ful argyments. Instead ob frettin' yo'selves inter
early graves fearin' dat yo' parients may come to some bad
end, jest hump yo'selves ober de problem ob gettin' in yo' nex
ton ob coal, an' larn how ter git a chicken off de perch wiv-

out makin' it squawk. Nebber try ter climb ober a fence wiv a watermellin unner each arm an' de farmer's dorg hangin' onter de back porch ob yo' trousaloons.

It am one ob de oncertainties ob life how anybody will turn out. De booful blue-eyed curly haired boy often grows up to be a two-cent dude, an' de snub-nosed, freckled-faced, lanky gal ob ten, often becomes a vision ob paralyzin' beauty, at eighteen. De biggest watermellin may be green, an' de fattest hen may be tougher'n tripe.

Darfore in conclusion let me resure yo' dat de bes' yo' can do am dat which appears to be mostly more so, or somewhat otherwisely, especially if it am no greater dan it would be ef it were lesser probably to de extent ob bein' de interior diameter compared to de triangle ob de circumstantial lumination. Hopin' yo' feel honored as yo' orter be, I take pleasure in wishin' yo' good-night. (*Exit*).

SPRING.

Enters wrapped in mufflers and wearing two or three overcoats. Removes wrappings as he speaks.

Ladies, Gemmen an' Feller Icicles:—Excuse me fo' a few minutes while I undo myself. De subject ob my remarks dis ebenin' am Spring. I announce it aforehand so dat yo' wont fink I hab sprung spring onter yo' too sudden.

Spring am come. De boundin' blizzard from Dakota eftsoon will gambol awayward toward de Norf Pole; and, lest de people get lonesome, de laughing cyclone will joyfully caper forth; an' right merrily will it gather up houses an' lots an' men an' mules an' cattle an' horses an' forty acre farms an' so forth, and scatter dem ober seventy counties.

Spring am come. De sad, holler-eyed poet issueth forth from his lair, an' warbleth: "Hail, Gentle Spring!" An' den verily doth it hail an' snow, an' blow an' sleet an' friz eben unto de fust ob June.

Den getteth de country roads heavy wiv red an' blue clay which sticketh closer dan a brudder; an' behold de mule driver cusseth an' humpeth hisself dat he getteth not stucketh in de mud. Yea, verily.

Spring am come. De car'less man walketh upon rotten ice an' tumbleth in, an' lifteth up his voice an' damneth his luck; an' de Dakota lion sheddeth four ob his overcoats an' remarketh dat de winter hab been berry mild.

Spring am come. De joyful plumber maketh out his bill fo' stoppin' a ten-cent leak in de pipe an' taketh the house itself in part payment.

De city gal buyeth a yard ob silk fo' a bathin' suit, an' de innercent country rustic layeth in a stock ob canned vegetables an' advertiseth "good country board" in de newspapers. Den he sitteth calmly down an' waiteth fo' de city sucker to come an' pay ten dollars a week fo' de fun ob sleepin' on a rocky bed, eatin' canned goods, an' bein' chawed by muskeeters.

Spring am come. De wise book-agent getteth de rear porch ob his pantaloons lined wiv copper an' bravely saileth forth, fo' verily he feareth de boot ob no man.

De base ball umpire hireth an ambitious young mule to kick him fourteen hours daily, letteth de cars run ober him a few times, drinketh Indiana whiskey, an' so tougheneth himself fo' de fray.

De editor lieth in ambush, where he loadeth his gun fo' spring poets, an' smileth to himself, an' sayeth, " Ha ! Ha !" as he chucketh in de buckshot.

Eftsoon de small boy eateth ob de green apple; an' behold ! In de still, silent hours ob de night de colic arriveth, an' climbeth upon him wiv bofe feet an' sluggeth him. And his wail am heard in de lan'.

Spring am come. She'll be here when she arroves.

(exit).

BUSINESS.

How de do, folkses? I don' see what you's laffin at. Can't a niggah say, " How do" wivout you sniggerin' in his face? I came here mindin' my own business, to talk about business, an' yo' has no business to laff at me. So now.

Fustly an' darfore foremostly in de fustest place, let us consider de king an' queen business. Folkes in dat line hab a hard time ob it. Fink ob pore ole Queen Victory an' all her trubble. Fink ob what a job she has wiv de Prince ob Wales allus gettin' inter debt an' slashin' erroun' wiv naughty actresses. See how she haster 'conemize an' go wivout sugar in her coffee jes' còs de blamed Britishers don't 'low her only a million dollars a year to live on. Its awful. See how de Cigar ob Russia haster dodge bomb-shells, etc., an' how he he haster hab a guard ob a thousand men ebbery time he goes out arter a bucket ob coal. See what a time de jim jam King ob Sweden has pullin' royal purple snakes an' sky-blue alligators out ob his boots. Pity, pity, de poor unhappy Sundown ob Turkey browsin' aroun' in a cold world wiv only two er free hundred wives to cheer his lonely way. No my frens, de king an' queen business don't pay. I know it don't. I bet all I had once on four kings an' it didn't pay—kase de udder feller had ace high—an' a razor.

I will now turn de electric light ob my fo'ty horse power intellect on de political business. Am dar a politician har to-night? Ef so I want to tell him dat he am standin' on de brink ob a volcano wat am liable ter blow him ter Jericho. When a man gets elected Constable er Justice ob de Peace, he finks he will be de nex' President ob de United States. But bress yo' soul, he wont. An' sposin' he did—what den? What den? Why, ef de mugwumps elected him, udder side would kick, an' ef de firemen voted fo' him to once, dar'd be saramcastic remarks erbout " Blocks ob Fires." Den he

must turn all de rascals out an' turn de udder rascals in, an'
no use talkin' he'd wish he'd died a hunnerd y'ars afore he
was bo'n.   Yes sah.   Look back at extemporaenous history
an' tole me whar de politicians· am now.   Whar am Julium
Ceasar?   Dead.   Wot killed him?   Politics.   Whar am
Mark Antony?   Dead.   Yet he was a fust-class stump
speaker.   He could get up on a dry goods box an' gib 'em
fits any day.   He had de newspapers all fixed, an' he stood
solid wiv de boys—uster take 'em on great 'scursions down
de ribber, wiv er brass band an' all de beer an' cigars dey
wanted.   He belonged to de Masons an' de Knights ob
Labor, de Mulligan Guards an' udder sercieties.   He
knowed ebbery barkeeper in Rome, an' yet, whar am he?
No sah.   Politics don't pay.   Yo' may sell yo' vote or come
in fo' a big swag, but de oppersition noospapers will get
hole ob it an' den yo' name will be Dennis.

Consid'rin all de pints, I fink dat farmin' am a fust-class
business; an' as I see one or two farmers concealed in pub·
lic to-night, I will gib dem de benefit ob my expectations.

Fustly to-wit: Co'n in de ear am apt to effect de hearin'.
Co'n on de foot makes yo' swar' ef somebody stomps on it.
Green co'n makes de voice husky, an' co'n juice am good
fo' bunions ef tooken internally.

Pumpkins am good fo' pies, but squashes make de bes'
pumpkin pies.   Besides, nobody will mistook yo' head fo' a
squash.

Nebber pick apples wiv a pick-ax.   It am apt to destroy
de vines.   And don't pare yo' apples wiv a parasol.   It wont do.

De bes' time to put in rye am jes' afore brexfus.   Some
farmers, 'specially dem livin' in de city, puts it in all day
an' half de night, but it's apt to make de head swell.

A good drain can be built by puttin' a heavy mortgage
on de farm.   Ef necessary repeat de dose, an' it will drain
yo' las' cent to pay de interest.

Nebber make cider except in de new ob de moon. Ef yo' do yo' am likely to get full afore yo' know it. Allers bile yo' cider ober a slow fire, rinse it out in clear water an' hang it on de fence to dry.

Do not, I beg ob yo', do not sow wheat wiv a sewing machine. An' don't use de baby crib to cradle yo' grain.

Late plowin' am usually better dan early plowin' as it gives de hired man a chance to sleep longer in de mornin'. But do not plow later dan twelve o'clock at night. Ef yo' do yo' gits de hosses inter de habit ob stayin' out late, an' besides it's bad fo' de plow. I hab known plows to get de whoopin' cough an' congestive rheumatism from late plow. in'. It's bad.

Do not argue wiv a sittin' hen. Let her sot. Ef yo' hab no eggs fo' her, sot her on door knobs.

De bes' way to raise chickuns am on a dark night. Grab 'em by de neck an' chuck em in a bag. Den dey wont holler.

An Alderney cow gibs de best milk, but chalk an' water am pow'ful handy.

Remember dat economy am de spice ob life. Darfore skim yo' milk car'fully on de top, turn it ober an' skim it on de bottom.

Pick yo' strawberries gently so as not to injure de straw, an' remember dat buckwheat am not good to eat, as it am liable to cake in de stomach.

It am up-hill work to raise pertaters, but yo' kin git a fine crop ob bugs wivout half tryin'.

In disclosin' my remarks I would say, dat de farmer orter get along, as he *cabbages* a good deal, is allers *thrashin'*, manages to *turnup* considerable an' *beets* some, to say nuffiin' o' raisin' his own celery (*salary*).

Hopin' I has *planted* some good ideas which will not *harrow* yo' feelins', I will dray myself off. (*exit*).

MATTERS AND THINGS.

WHITE PEOPLE AND UDDER FOLKESES:—In addressin'
yo' dis ebbenin' I finds myself under de dense necessity ob
concludin' dat I orter say suffin, ef not more so.

To return to my subject. A great many people am more
or less different from udder people, who am different from
dem. Dat's so an' more so.

When in de course ob inhuman events it becomes necessary fo' a man to eliminate de constructive difference from
de planetary problem, what objective dissolution am de
ebberlastin' screech ob a lonesome Thomas cat got ter do
wiv de brickbat flung at him? Dat's so an' more so.

How long am a ribber? How deep am a well? How
big am a house? How short am a piece ob rope?

Who kin tell why grass am green instead ob yaller? Who
invented de Rocky Mountains? Whar did Mary get her
little lamb, an' who wrote de "Beautiful Snow?" Who
struck Billy Patterson, an' why does a dog turn aroun'
afore layin' down? Don't anser ef yo' can't.

Almost any man am pore enuff ter own *one* dog. Some
men are pore enuff ter own six.

When de sun rises airly an' sots late de days am longer
dan udderwise. Dat's so an' more so too.

A man may be pore as de hind leg ob Job's turkey, but
bimeby he invents a new kind ob chawin' gum an' gits rich
an' flies to de top ob de fence, de biggest toad in de
puddle.

Yo' see stars on a clear night, an' yo' also see 'em in de
daytime ef yo' stop a man's fist wiv yo' nose, er fool eround
de business end ob a mule. *Dat's* so an' more so too.

De sun lights de day, an' de man who tumbles down
sta'rs, lights on his head, or somewhar else. An' de
luminary conglomerations which dissolves eround creation,
express de sensibility ob de sun, moon, stars, planets an'

comets dat am up above de *world* so high, like a muskeeter on an elephant's back.

To return to my subject (*loudly*): In de nex' place, we must consider ef de roly poly am a component abstraction ob de house dat Jack built, or de limination ob de interior outside.

To return to my subject: Ef it was not fo' women whar would we be? We owe a great deal to women, includin' board bills, to say nuffin ob washin' an' ironin'. Dat's so, an' more so.

I am berry fond ob music, but I am no songist. I am allers sad when I sing, an' so am dem what hears me. Some songs am berry disappropriate. For instance, it riles up a man when he's drivin' er balky mule, ter hear a feller warble, " Listen to my Tale ob Whoa." When Ise strollin' eround a watermellin patch arter dark, I don't like ter h'ar a feller sing, " Johnny get yo' gun." It sounds pussonal. When an Irishman slips down on a banahner skin, he wants ter fought ef somebody yells, " Down Went McGinty," an' when I goes out wearing a new beaver, I wants ter use a razor ef anybody asks me whar I got dat hat.

I doesn't car' a cent fo' money. I only trabbles aroun' ter see de world an' exhibit my store clothes. Dat's so, an' more so.

I is berry fond ob art. I like pictures. I like ter draw. I once drawed a fifty-cent turkey at a raffle, an' it cost me fo'r dollars to pay fo' de congratulations—includin' beer.

To return to my subject: Time passes on. Time is allers passin' mo' or less. It's suffin I nebber does—ef I has a good hand. Dis calls up a sad question. Whar am de gals ob my youthful youth? Some is married, an' some wanter be. Dose dat am wish dey wasn't. Dose dat aint wish dey was. Some people am nebber happy.

I once knowed a man in New Jarsey wot hadn't a single

toof in his head—nor eben a double toof. An' strange to say, he had none in his mouf. It sometimes happens dat way. Yet, in spite ob it, dat man could play de cymbals in a louder key dan any man I ebber seed.

I once staid into a hotel whar dey was short ob pillers, so dey gib me a bag ob oats fo' to rest my weary head. I nad de night mares awful. In de mornin' de landlord axed me, "How does yo' feel ole hoss—*hey*? Sez I, " I feel my oats, sah." Dat's so, an' mo' so too. (*exit*).

A CELEBRATED WOMAN.

FRIENDS AND CITIZEN FELLOWS:—Sometime ago I was in Bosting, an' arter dining wiv de Governor we went to a meetin' ob de Serciety ob Culchaw, whar I listened to a lecture an de subject ob " Little Jack Horner" who sat in a corner. It was very touchin'. It drew tears from my eyes, and a dollar from my pocket. Arter I got home I cooled my fevered brow an' sot down an' writ de lecture which I shall inflict on yo' to-night. De subject ob my discourse am a famous female woman of which you may have heard—de late lamented Mrs. Hubbard. A great poet hab spoke ob her as follers:

> Old Mother Hubbard,
> Went to de cupboard
> To get her pore dorg a bone.
> When she got there
> De cupboard was bare,
> An' so de pore dorg got none.

What a world ob pathetic pathos am concealed in dese above aforesaid spoken lines.

As yo' will observe, Mrs. Hubbard was *old*. Probably she was a woman. In dat case, she was an old woman, an' no doubt a female besides. This makes it all de sadder. Excuse me while I weep (*wipes eyes with very large handkerchief*).

But, my friends, did Mrs. Hubbard despair? Did she kerflumex? Did she sot down an' wail an' wope an' read one ob Howell's novels or chew gum? No sah! Not her. *She went to de cupboard.*

Now consider dis pint. She *went.* She did not call de cupboard to her, but she went. How? In what way? Did she go on a bicycle or roller skates or a toboggan? Alas, we know not. Perhaps she walked. Who can tell.

Nextly, to continue, and furthermore besides, to-wit: *Why* did she go to de cupboard? Did she go arter golden store, rich mine, silver spoons, arple sass, diamonds, shot guns or a seal skin sack? (*loudly*) *No!* She went to get her pore dorg a bone.

I regret to inform yo' dat I cannot inform yo' what kind ob bone she seeked to bone from de cupboard. It might hab been a fish-bone or a wish-bone, a jaw-bone, ham-bone or a trombone. It was a bone, anyhow, for her pore dorg, who, being pore, probably was not rich. He may have had *scent* or two. Most dorgs do, sometimes. Dis, however, am a dogmatic digression.

When she got there
De cupboard was bare.

Think ob it! Arter her long an' weary journey across de room to de cupboard, it was bare. Dat am to say, so to speak, dat nuffin was in it. In udder words, it was empty. She found no ham-bone, no boned turkey, no baked beans, nor biled onions, no pie nor cake. Dar' was no quail on toast, no pickled eel's feet, no biled hen's teeth, no turnups nor turn downs, no ice cream, no nuffin.

An' so de pore dorg had none.

None what? None anything. Being as it was bare, it was empty an' so contained nuffin, or at least not anything muchly as it were, so to speak.

Probably she saw or observed, or at all events mentioned de cold, hard, stern fact dat being as de cupboard was bare de dorg would hab to skirmish around for grub. Perhaps. Perhaps not so much.

De question now arises to a somewhat moreso or less degree, what did Mrs. Hubbard do, an' also de dorg? Did she sot down an' sob, an' did he go out and howl at de moon or chase a cat? Also we know not what.

From dis great moral lesson let us apply some facts ob considerable or somewhat greater interest.

Don't keep yo' bones in an empty cupboard.

Don't go to de cupboard an' get a bone when it aint dar.

Don't keep a dorg what wants bones. Git one dat prefers buckwheat pancakes with maple syrup.

Above all things, learn to apply to yo'selves dis great poem:

> Hey diddle diddle, de cat an' de fiddle,
> De cow jumped ober de moon,
> De little dorg laughed to see de sport,
> An' de dish run away wiv de spoon.

My friends, I has one more expressive thing to say, an' dat is good-night. (*exit*).

NATURE.

LADIES AND ALSO GENTLEMEN: I am going to address you to-night on a natural subject, and that subject is Nature. I will not touch de sun, moon nor stars. I could not reach them if I wanted to, and I would probably burn my fingers if I did.

Therefore I will confine my remarks to the animal king-dom, which will be quite easy as many of the animal kingdom are confined—in jails and such like.

Man of course stands first among the animal kingdom, except when he is under the influence of liquor. Then he is

apt to lie. Some men lie when they are *not* under the influence of liquor.

Mankind, and also men who are not kind, differ from
other animals in several respects. Man is the only animal
that laughs. I sometimes indulge in a "smile" myself.
Did some one ask me to "have something?" Alas, no. I
see it was only a dream. Man is the only animal that chews
tobacco, drinks torchlight whiskey or plays on the violin.
For this let us be truly thankful.

There are a great many races, including the negro race,
the Indian race, boat-race, horse-race and foot-race. I ran a
foot-race once myself, and won easily. The sheriff was too
fat, so I got away.

Dogs are found everywhere. The poorer a man is, the
more he has. The dog-star is not a dog. Neither is the
dog-fish nor dog-wood. Cats are also numerous, especially
on moonlight nights. The cat is a beautiful singer, but his
voice needs cultivating. A double barrel shot-gun improves
it wonderfully.

The sheep is sometimes a blackleg, but he gambols only
on the green—grass. The hydraulic ram is not a gentleman
sheep, as some suppose. Neither is the sheeps-head.

Cows are chiefly grown for the purpose of making cow-
hide boots. Some unprincipled men adulterate water with
cow's milk. This is very wrong. Water should never be
reduced with anything but whiskey, and the proportion
should be one part of water to ninety-six parts of whiskey.
Irish bulls do not belong to the cow race. Neither did
Sitting Bull. I will not speak of calves. It might be considered somewhat indelicate. Besides, I did not come here
to make any personal allusions. I see an escaped dude in
the audience, and he might object.

Deer are very graceful animals. Young men find
them very expensive when they become addicted to the ice

cream or oyster habit. I knew a little dear who could eat seven plates of ice cream and sigh for more.

The horse belongs to the equine class. Very often he belongs to the three minute class. A bucking horse bucks. So does a saw-buck. That's a horse on me. I did not intend to *saddle* a joke on you, so I will *bridle* my tongue. I spoke on the *spur* of the moment. Keep your seats. I have a *horse* pistol here which I raised from a *colt*. So beware. A colt is much like a lazy man. He will do no work until he's broke.

Bears are found in the woods, and also in Wall street. The latter are by far the most dangerous. If you meet a lady bear walking out with her children, you better run, or there will be trouble bruin.

Elephants and tigers are found chiefly in large cities. Men very often "see the elephant" and "buck the tiger." Both are very expensive pastimes. I know it. Don't ask me how.

Beavers are made from beaver hats. They are quite profane, although they seldom dam anything but rivers

The alligator has a very open countenance, but you are apt to be taken in if you become too familiar with him. Turtles are used for soup—especially mock turtles. They are not celebrated for speed, but give them time, and they will go quite a ways. The largest weighs the most.

Fish are good for the brain. Some day I will capture a dude and feed him a whale three times a day. Perhaps in time the germ of a brain may appear. Fish are caught in various ways. The largest always get away. Use plenty of bait when you go fishing. I always carry a quart of the best. Man resembles fish in many respects. Some are sharks, some are bull heads, and many are rum—suckers.

Birds are quite well known. They are chiefly used to disfigure women's hats—which are worn so that people sitting behind them can't see. A highly valuable bird is the American eagle, which is worth exactly ten dollars. The hen is used to scratch up your neighbor's garden, and the rooster's chief purpose is to wake you up in the morning by crowing under your window. Therein he differs from the crow, which does *not* crow, although we know he has *caws.* It is true that one swallow does not make a summer but some are made drunk by swallowing strong drink.

Snakes are not pleasant companions. They are cold blooded, and apt to be reserved. The black snake is sometimes used as a whip, and the adder is handy for a bookkeeper. Snakes are found everywhere. I have known some men to see them, even in their mind's eye. When a man finds snakes in his boots he ought to sign the pledge.

Among the numerous bugs known to mankind are the humbug, the big-bug, and another, which shall be nameless. The flea is a lively bird. I once heard a minister remark that "the wicked flee where no man pursueth." I think he may have had no experience.

The fly is the present tense of the flee. However, he is too well known to require description. Therefore as I have exhausted my subject and your patience, I will fly before it becomes necessary to flee. I thank you all and no doubt you are glad of it. Good-night. (*exit*).

TEMPERANCE ORATION.

FELLOW SINNERS: As I hab a number ob people ter see ter night, I trust yo' will none of yo' go outer see a man afore I finish my brief remarks.

Friends an' feller imbibers, I stan' afore yo' dis yer night as a frightful example ob de perpetuation ob strong drink.

For years an' years, if not longer, I crooked de elbow an' looked upon de wine when it was red, an' de gin when it was white. I lost all my money an' finally got so poor dat I couldn't get trusted eben fo' a drink, as de barkeepers said dey could see right through me.

Finally when de world looked as dark as de bottom ob a coal mine ter me, I jined a temp'rance serciety. Look at de result. I am no longer poor. I lib on de fat ob de land. I wear store clothes an' hab been able to git in debt all over town. I has got so used ter being dunned dat I feels insulted ef a man meets me an' don't ax me ter settle dat little bill.

Dat's what temp'rance has done fo' me. Go thou ole feller boozer an' do likewise also.

My fren's, dar am a sarpent in ebbery glass, an' ef yo' insist on drinkin' yo' will presently soon find a whole flock ob sarpents in yo' boots.

What am liquor? It am something yo' puts into your brain to steal away your stummick.

What am it made of? Oh, my lushin' friends jes wait until I tole yo'. Hang onter yo'self now.

Liquor am made ob alcohol, Paris green, oil ob vit'rol, benzine, arsenic, lemons, sugar, hot water, etc., de last bein' required in makin' dat delightful but seductive decoction known as punch.

What am de effects ob drinkin' liquor? Dar am quite a number. Fust yo' gets drunk. Den yo' wants to fought. Den yo' gets licked, an' den yo' gits ten dollar or thirty days. I uster git thirty days twice a month.

Dat am one effect. Anudder effect am dat yo' git drunk, go home an' tell yo' wife yo' is been to de lodge, an' git Hail Columbia Happy Land an' a rollin' pin ober de head. I has had my head rolled out flat as a pancake many a time, so dat I could hardly squoze it back inter shape. Anyhow, my hat wouldn't fit in de mornin'.

Still anudder effect am dat yo' git drunk, roll around in

de gutter, spile yo' clothes, ruin yo' good looks an' wind up by bein' wound up with a fine assortment ob bright red jim jams an' royal purple snakes.

Oh, my friends, fink ob all de money a man spends for liquor, eben ef he do get trusted. Somebody has to pay fo' it, an' ef de drinker don't, de pore saloonist must. In dat case his wife may be compelled, actually compelled, to wear her last year's diamonds dis year an' git along wiv only three or four sealskin sacques.

Think of this my feller imbiberates an' shun de flowing bowl as you would shun de man to whom you owe five dollars.

Drink nothing but water. Water am free onless you live in cities having water taxes. Water am de friend of man, 'specially de milkman.

Whiskey was nebber made to drink onless yo' has chil'-blains, or has interviwed a rattlesnake.

Water am pure an' harmless, an' hurts nobody. Darfore drink water.

As I was sayin' (*takes flask from pocket*). Yo' needn't laugh. I is not goin' to take a smile. Dis bottle contains cough syrup· I rode inter town on a pony, so am a little *ho*(*a*)*rse* (*drinks*). As I was sayin', whisky am de foe of all mankind. It am only fit to be put down (*drinks*). So great am my aversion to de vile stuff dat I am allers glad ter help put it down (*drinks*). Oh, my friends, break off dis habit while yet dar is time, an' remember—ic—what a frightful *drinks*,) *and acts tipsy*) frightful zample—ic—it am fo' a man to get drunk. Water am all right for puttin' out fires (*drinks*). But wa—water drowns folks an' whisky—whoo! whisky don't. My friends—ic—er—beware of water. It biteth like a sarpent, an' stingeth like an adder. My frens—ic—I'm sorry to say yo' all seem to be 'toxicated (*reels*) what fo' am yo' reeling about so? My frens Ise

'fraid you'll sot me a bad zample. I gwine out ter see a
man. Go' night. (*upsets table, and reels out*).

MANKIND.

LADIES AND GENTLEMEN: Man is an animal who lives
mostly on the earth, though sometimes he lives on his wife's
relatives.

There is quite a variety of men, including good men, bad
men, John L. Sullivan and the President of the United
States. There is also the man in the moon.

The *good* man is all right unless he is *too* good. Then
look out for him. Some of these dreadfully good men are
philanthropists. They send rum, missionaries and red
flannel undergarments to Africa, and cut down the wages
of their workmen as soon as the tariff is raised. They give
money to churches, and turn their tenants out of doors in
midwinter if they are a day behind in their rent. I always
long for a club when I see such men.

The *mean* man isn't fit to live. He spends a dollar for
cigars and gives his wife twenty-five cents to buy a new
dress. He would give his little boy a penny, then steal it
from him and whip him for losing it.

The hypocrite is the meanest man in the world. Sometimes he is a pious fraud who draws his mouth down and
rolls his eyes up, and talks through his nose. He goes to
church four times on Sunday, and robs his fellow creatures
the other six days.

The *fidgety* man is always in a hurry. He is always going
somewhere, and usually misses his train. He is very for-
getful and loses his head whenever excited. He wants to
talk about *himself* whenever you want to talk about *yourself*, and he is dead set against noise. If your darling little
boy stands on his front steps and yells or beats a drum or

tries to have any innocent fun, the fidgety man objects. The young man next door, who is learning to blow the cornet or play the violin is his pet aversion, and he even goes so far as to get mad when the poor, harmless pussy-cats hold a convention in his back yard.

The *eccentric* man is not popular. He has a disgusting habit of telling the truth. He has been known to tell a fond young mother that her little popsy wopsy baby was no more wonderful than any other baby—and only escaped with his life because murder is illegal.

The *fast* man is always *loose*—strange as it may seem. He is always good to his relatives. He often gives his "uncle" some valuable article to keep, and he is very fond of his "ante." He delights in hunting, and will *poker* round for game, but never does it unless he has money for his *ante*. That is why I know he is fond of her.

The *lazy* man loves to sit on a drygoods box and manage the government while he whittles a soft pine stick. He is never too tired to eat, but he abhors any labor that requires him to work. He always puts off to-day what he knows he wont do to-morrow. He will probably die some day if he lives long enough, because he is too tired to breathe.

The *dude* is one-fourth man and four-thirds fool. His number four hat covers an empty space where his brain ought to be. The dude wears outlandish clothing, a large walking stick, and an idiotic smile. He is too stupid to argue, too idiotic to think, and too insignificant to thrash. I always kick a dude when I meet him the same as I do his brother, the poodle pup. Of the two I respect the poodle the most. He cannot help being a cur, and the dude might help being a jackass, if he would.

The *jolly* man is the best fellow in the world. His wife adores him, his children love him, and the whole world is glad to see him. He looks on the bright side of everything and smiles, even when he has the toothache. He always laughs at your stories, no matter how stupid they are, and he does not get mad if you do not agree with him in religion and politics. He has a kind word for everybody, and he never gives a poor man the worst of a deal. He may have trouble, but he doesn't whine about it, and he is always ready to help a man who is down in his luck. He minds his own business, never pokes his nose into other people's affairs, and never sneaks around saying dirty things behind a person's back. He is not very numerous, I am sorry to say, but I hope everybody within the sound of my voice will try to emulate him. That's all. (*exit*).

PROF. WHANG'S ORATION.

FELLER CITIZENS: I want yo' ter sot still an' try, try hard to let yo' minds—ef yo' has any—dwell onto de remarks dat I am about to turn loose.

Feller citizens, we is livin' in a monumental an' awful period of time. We come up as a sunflower an' am cut down like er watermellin.

De ebberlastin' jim slicker has knocked de bottom outer all creation, an' de bangdoodle sots on de back fence mouruin' fo' his lost kibosh. It's enuff ter fotch tears to de eyes of a dead grindstone, muchly more so, to-wit, *et cetera*, and so forth.

Feller citizens, our good ship of state am sloshin' about in de waters of tribulation, an' will go to Kingdom Come onless we haw gee her off de rocks an' bring her eroun' like a sottin' hen on a cold day in August.

Whar am de tariff? Who am got it hid erway in his trousaloon's pocket? I would go on a *tariff* I had him by de nape ob de neck.

Let us peer inter de dim future like a hungry tramp hustlin' fo' hash, er a bobtail mugwump poodle dorg chasing de place whar his tail orter be. *Yes sah!*

Whar, in de name ob all de bygone glories ob Bunker Hill, am de glorious Bird of Liberty dat flewed away on de wings ob de mornin' beyond the whenceness, to de polywog ob de future ? Let echo anser ef she dar'.

An' dat reminds me ob de results ob danger, an' recalls de bootiful poem wot goes as follers:

> Oh, I sigh fo' a sight ob my dear wiggy wee,
> Who libs at de fut ob de skiddymadee.
> Has de fierce bolly goggle, kagoozled my love ?
> Am she scar'd inter fits by de wild muggy huv ?
> Oh, slamity—bangity, blood in my eye,
> Oshkosh and Jerusalem—*root hog er die.*

Feller citizens, nuffin am like what it was afore it changed from what it was afore it was different.

Shall dis great nation which extends from de Rockalgany mountains to de udder side ob Jerdon be skewjawed outer shape an' squegeed like a one-eyed shanghai rooster tryin' ter pick a corn from de hind fut ob a one-legged *man* ?

Shall de whole yankee nation, which licked all creation, an' won a high station, bust up wiv inflation, an go ter tarnation on dis yar occasion. *No sah!*

Den let us unite an' pull togedder like a porous plaster. An', finally, hen de lion an' de lamb lay down togedder an' de conniption fits am knocked galley west, an' de little dorg laffs to see de sport while de cow jumps ober de moon, so ter spoke—den, an' den only, will de outside curve ob de diameter dance a jig wiv de milky way, an' de all-fired glorious bird ob liberty will flop her wings an' crow, sayin', *E. pluribust onion, root hog er die.*

Pounds table with umbrella, then tips over table and falls under it as curtain descends.

LECTURE ON THE HOG.

My friends, there are two kinds of hogs in this world. The first has four feet—the other, two. Of the former I will speak first.

I do not know who discovered the hog. He probably existed in prehistoric times. He may have been in Eden, but that is doubtful, as Satan did not enter into him for a long time afterwards. Besides a mud-puddle is a hog's paradise and I think there were none in Eden.

However, there is no doubt that a hog got into the ark, at all events, Noah took Ham into the ark with him.

The hog is composed of head, body, tail and a large voice. Hogsheads are chiefly employed for holding molasses. The tail is more ornamental than useful; indeed, it is good for nothing, so far as I can see, except to show where the hog leaves off.

The voice of the hog is a high soprano, and sounds much like a buzz saw quarreling with a railroad spike.

When the owner of this voice is hungry—and he is never anything else—his voice will cause a locomotive whistle to hide its diminished head, and even the song of the Thomas cat cannot drown it.

The hog is blessed with an excellent appetite, and is not at all particular regarding his diet. True he does not prefer tin cans and circus bills like the goat, but he will go at things which the latter would not touch.

Down South they have invented a style of hog known as the razor-back. He can outrun any horse, and even the fiery, untamed locomotive has to snort to catch him. Necessity has made the Southern hog fleet of foot, as he is often obliged to indulge in footraces with impecunious darkeys, whose mouths water for bacon.

The hog is always trying experiments. He has no idea of his own size. I saw a large hog waste a great deal of time and much bad language trying to work his way through a small auger-hole in the fence, and yet when his owner wanted him to go through an open gate he pretended it was not large enough.

The hog noses around a good deal. I suppose that is what his nose is for.

The hog does not care much for style, and he is not at all amiable. He is not refined and his language at times is shocking.

He is a great traveler. Even when he is salted down and apparently cured of wandering, he will sometimes get up in the dead of the night, go some distance and hide a part of himself in some man's empty barrel.

The two-footed swine is much worse than his brother, for he pretends to be a man.

This variety of hog is very disgusting. When he eats he guzzles and champs and smacks, making a noise like a thrashing-machine. Usually he eats with his knife instead of his fork, poking it into his mouth until you hope that he will cut his throat. But no such good luck ever happens.

In traveling the brutish instincts of the human hog shine forth most brilliantly. He always wants two seats in a car, and will take four if he can get them. Elderly people and weary women may stand, but the human swine cares nothing for that.

He is a gross, vulgar coward, always ready to bully or insult helpless women or children; but let a man appear and he instantly becomes a very tame hog.

Do you know such a specimen? Of course you do, for he is found everywhere. Then look at him, study him, detest him, and then vow you will never become one of his class.

Don't be a clam, but of all things don't, *don't*, DON'T be a hog. (*exit*).

NEGRO PLAYS.

Many successful plays have popular negro characters in the cast, yet they cannot be used for minstrel entertainments.

Therefore, plays should be selected from the regular Ethiopian Drama. These plays are short, lively, full of brisk fun, and all are easily presented.

Usually it is preferable to select plays where no female characters appear. But in all of the following described plays, the female characters may be assumed by males. In such cases let me warn the amateur against indulging in any action displaying the least trace of vulgarity.

In playing a female role, even in a negro farce, it is better to under-act than over-act. Of course the dress may be somewhat *outré* and the gestures exaggerated, but coarseness must be strictly forbidden.

In regular minstrel companies all the characters are played with black faces. I advise amateurs to follow this rule, as a white-face character in a negro minstrel entertainment is decidedly out of place.

The following list is classified, showing the number of characters, scenery, plat, time of playing, etc. Copies may be purchased from the publisher of this book, at the uniform price of 15 cents each, by mail postpaid.

TWO MALE CHARACTERS.

THE HAUNTED HOUSE.

A favorite farce played with much success by the Christy Minstrels. *Mr. Livingston* hires *Pete* to do a job of whitewashing. *Pete* pretends to be very brave, but is badly frightened by "ghosts." Scene, plain room. Time, eight minutes. The "ghosts" are represented by a number of characters in white sheets.

STOCKS UP, STOCKS DOWN.

A ludicrous scene between a hard-up "author" and his friend. Full of comical business. Scene, a street or plain room. Time, eight minutes.

DEAF—IN A HORN.

A negro musician has a pupil who pretends to be very deaf. A popular farce on the professional stage, and full of laughable business. Scene, plain room. Time, ten minutes.

HANDY ANDY.

One of the funniest farces ever written for this number of characters. *Old Grimes* a quick-tempered old darkey hires *Andy* to work for him. *Andy* is full of mischief and keeps *Old Grimes* in continual torment. Scene, plain room. Time, fifteen minutes.

OTHELLO AND DESDEMONA.

A roaring burlesque on the "chamber scene" from "Othello." *Jake* and *Pete*, a couple of stranded "actors" undertake to do a scene from "Othello," and never fail to bring down the house. Plain room scene. Time, twelve minutes.

ALL EXPENSES.

A theatrical manager is looking for an actor. He engages *Jemius*. He then endeavors to instruct him, and a very laughable scene ensues. Exterior scene. Time, ten miuutes.

THREE MALE CHARACTERS.

BACK FROM CALIFORNY.

A very laughable farce, loaded with comical business. *Dr. Squozzle* and *Zip Johnson* are waiting for a train. They get into a roaring row, making things hot for *Cuffee*, the waiter, and finally discover that they are brothers-in-law. Scene, a plain room. Time, twelve minutes.

SPORTS ON A LARK.

A couple of "dead beat" darkeys try to get the best of a "dude." But the "dude" happens to be a lively bird, and gives them all they want—and more too. Very lively, and sure to please. Scene, exterior. Time, eight minutes.

QUARRELSOME SERVANTS.

One of the most popular and successful negro farces ever written. Brimful of bright fun. A peaceable old man hires a couple of servants, making each promise not to quarrel. Instead of keeping their word, they get into a regular free fight, and the old man comes in for a share of the trouble. Interior scene. Time, ten minutes.

THE DARKY TRAGEDIAN.

Considered by many to be the best of all the negro farces. A stage struck darkey, his calculating friend and a sleepy "coon" get up a scene from "Romeo and Juliet," which always creates roars of laughter. Each character is first-class, and the situations are side-splitting. Interior scene. Time, fifteen minutes.

AN UNHAPPY PAIR.

A couple of "dead broke" and very hungry "coons" try

to get a square meal out of a musician. Their numerous tricks and schemes are very laughable. Scene, exterior. Time, ten minutes. A few extra characters are required to represent a band.

VARIOUS CHARACTERS.

STAGE STRUCK DARKEY.

Two male, one female characters. A laughable burlesque on tragic acting. A lively couple endeavor to frighten a country darkey by giving scenes from various plays. Some very laughable scenes follow. Interior scene. Time, ten minutes.

THE SHAM DOCTOR.

Four male, two female characters. *Liverheel*, finding that sawing wood is unprofitable, turns doctor. He practices on *Old Johnson* and some indescribably funny business follows. One exterior, two interior scenes. Time, fifteen minutes.

NO CURE, NO PAY.

Three male, one female character. *Dr. Ipecac* mistakes his daughter's lover for a deaf and dumb patient on whom he wishes to try a new theory. Very ludicrous blunders result, and the climax is a screamer. Interior scene. Time, ten minutes.

THE TWO POMPEYS.

Four male characters. A very funny rough-and-tumble farce, in which the comic business is evenly divided. Always successful on the professional stage, and very popular with amateurs.

PROF. BLACK'S FUNNYGRAPH.

Six male characters, with a few other darkeys on the stage to represent an audience. This is a darkey burlesque on the phonograph, and just bubbles over with fun. The *Professor's* "lecture" will bring down the house, and *Abe's* indignation at the impudence of the "funnygraph" is side-splitting. Easily produced. Interior scene. Time, fifteen minutes.

NOTE.—For other Ethiopian and miscellaneous plays see Denison's Catalogue.

NOTHING BETTER THAN THE SCRAP-BOOK RECITATION SERIES.

BY H. M. SOPER.

PRICE, POST PAID, PAPER, 25 CENTS.

"The selections are choice in quality and in large variety."—*Inter-Ocean*, Chicago.
"It excels anything we have seen for the purpose."—*Eclectic Teacher.*
"The latest and best things from our popular writers appear here."—*Normal Teacher.*

CONTENTS OF NO. 1.

T. S. DENISON, Publisher,

163 Randolph St., - - CHICAGO.

NOTHING BETTER

THAN THE SCRAP-BOOK RECITATION SERIES

BY H. M. SOPER.

ALL SORTS OF GOOD THINGS.

CONTENTS OF NO. 2.   PRICE POST-PAID, PAPER, 25 CENTS

T. S. DENISON, Publisher,
163 Randolph Street, CHICAGO.

NEW AMATEUR PLAYS.

Price 15 Cents Each, Postpaid.

☞ These plays are for schools and amateurs who have little or no scenery or stage conveniences. They contain nothing which cannot be presented in parlor, schoolroom or hall. They are ingenious in plot, entertaining in incident, and so easy in presentation that no society, however little experienced, can fail to make them at all times highly entertaining. *They are pure in tone and language.*

"The tone of these plays is good. Their moral is healthful."—*Pacific School and Home.*
"I have tested your plays and find them the best I have ever used in thirty terms of school."—*Ruth Haynes, Henrietta, O.*
"Your plays are new and novel, and admirably adapted to the use of amateurs."—*W. O. Dyke, West Gorham, Me.*
"Your plays seem to grow better."—*M. L. Spooner, Canaseraga, N. Y.*

ODDS WITH THE ENEMY.

A drama in 5 acts, by T. S. Denison; 7 m., 4 f. Time, 2 h. *Scenes:* A handsome parlor, and poor room. *Characters:* Heartless shark, dandy, darky comedian, a retired officer, and a private soldier, leading lady, soubrette, Yankee domestic. etc. This is an excellent play when well presented. Its tone is first-class, and it is sure to please.
"It took splendidly. Tabbs made it spicy."—*C. E. Rogers, Dunkirk, Ind.*

SETH GREENBACK.

A drama in 4 acts, by T. S. Denison; 7 m., 3 f. Time, 1 h., 15 m. *Scenes:* Parlor, room in a hotel. Irish comedian, Irish domestic, soubrette, leading lady, old man, villains. Seth Greenback fraudulently withheld his brother's portion of the paternal estate, excusing himself on the ground that the latter was a profligate spendthrift. The brother steals Seth's only son. By a strange fatality the little fellow is abandoned, and is taken in unknown to Seth, who treats him harshly. In a burglary of the house the boy is shot, and the secret is discovered. Very interesting throughout, and a great favorite.
"Seth Greenback was a perfect success. It can't be beat as an amateur drama."—*Will H. Tabbott, Coatesville, Ind., Dramatic Club.*

THE ASSESSOR.

A humorous sketch, by T. S. Denison; 3 m., 2 f. Time, 10 m. Illustrating the difficulties of the assessor in listing the property of Mr. Taxshirk, a farmer. Owing to the indiscretion of "Bub" and "Sairy Jane," the assessor catches the "bul kit." Very amusing.

BORROWING TROUBLE.

A farce by T. S. Denison; 3 m., 5 f. Time 20 m. Contains philanthropic gent who is a dead beat, old lady gossip, darky servant girl, doctor, detective. *Scene:* A plain room. This play illustrates the amusing experiences of a borrowing family. Some mustard in borrowed milk causes "strange feelings," and raises a ludicrous cholera excitement in the family.
"Borrowing Trouble fully sustained the excellent reputation gained by its author. It brought down the house."—*Madison (Wis.) Democrat.*

HANS VON SMASH.

A roaring farce in a prologue and one act, by T. S. Denison; 4 m., 3 f. Time, 30m. Hans, a "fresh" Dutchman; Katie, Irish domestic; Mr. Prettyman, too pretty to live; practical young ladies. etc. *Scene:* Plain room in a farmhouse. It has been rendered again and again all over the United States, and is always in demand. It will bear repeating every year.
Hans Von Smash is No 1, and no mistake."—*J. J. Flahiff, Helena, Ark.*
"Our Literary Association has presented upward of fifty dramas and farces, but never had any like like that."—*Secretary Chelmsford Center (Mass.) Literary Association.*

OUR COUNTRY.

A patriotic drama in three parts, by T. S. Denison; requires 10 m., 3 f. (Admits 11 m., 15f.) Time, 1 to 1½ hrs. Based on the Colonial and Revolutionary history of the United States. Costumes may be all made cheap at home. *Characters:* Brother Jonathan, John Bull, young ladies representing thirteen colonies, American, British and French officers, darky, Indians, etc. Tableaux: Indian attack, Burning of Stamp Act, Continental Soldier and Guardian Angel, Offerings of Peace. *Scenes:* Interior of log cabin, plain room, a picket post, Gen. Marion's tent, a street.
"Our Country took so well, that we repeated it to a crowded house."—*Nel Sweeney, Winslow, Ill.*

WANTED, A CORRESPONDENT.

A farce in 2 acts, by T. S. Denison; 4 m., 4 f. Time, 45 m. Middle-aged business man, young man, coachman, lively young ladies, and darky servant girl. A misunderstanding about an advertisement for a correspondent leads to amusing complications, and very unexpected results.

THE SCHOOL MA'AM.

A brilliant comedy in 4 acts, by T. S. Denison; 6 m., 5 f. Time, 1 h , 45m. *Characters:* Irish janitor, a good Mrs. Gamp and her little son," a self-made man (poor job), a bold, scheming, young woman, a director who always "agrees with the board," and a plucky "school ma'am." *Scenes:* Plain room, and interior of a schoolhouse. Nearly every incident in it is based on facts. It presents the ludicrous features of our schools admirably without offence to any. The Friend of Education, Mrs. Gamp and her ' little son," ond the janitor will wreck the gravity of any audience By all means try this; it is not for schools alone, but it is capital for good amateur clubs.

"It contains many good hits, and will be enjoyed by everybody."—*Educational Weekly.*
"It took to perfection."—*J. W. Jarnigan, Lynnville, Iowa.*

THE IRISH LINEN PEDDLER.

A capital farce in 2 acts, by T. S. Denison; 3 m., 3 f Time, 40 m Irish comedian, middle-aged man, young man, a scheming widow, young lady, Irish servant girl. *Scenes:* Room in farm house, and room in a hotel. The action of this farce is lively, the incidents unexpected and ludicrous. Pat O'Doyle, the peddler, is a combination of wit, drollery and impudence He will keep the house in high good humor. Easy of presentation and affords fine opportunities for acting. No poor character in the piece.

"The Irish Linen Peddler cannot be excelled in wit and humor. It kept the whole house in an uproar of laughter."—*T. J. Loar, Towanda, Ill.*

THE KANSAS EMIGRANTS.

A hilarious farce in two scenes, by T. S. Denison; 5 m., 1 f. Time, 20 m *Scene:* Interior of a shanty in Kansas. Contains two darky "Exodusters," early settler and wife, cow boy (to make up as an Indian), and a Boston swell. The incidents of this little play are so natural, yet so ludicrous that it must be seen to be appreciated. The way in which things get mixed, and the result of a practical joke will convulse any audience, no matter how solemn, and act on the liver more certainly than Podophyllin.

"Don't want anything better than The Kansas Immigrants "—*H. S. Kiehle, Circleville, Pa.*

TOO MUCH OF A GOOD THING.

A rattling comedy-farce, by T. S. Denison; 3 m., 6 f. Time, 45 m *Characters:* A precise step-mother, and five young ladies in training, who are inclined to make mischief, a country bumpkin, precise young man, old gent, full of sly humor. *Scene:* a parlor. Characters nearly all good. Tom Perkins, the bumpkin, will bring down the house. and keep it down. This play was prepared expressly for clubs, where female talent preponderates. It is a great favorite, as its large sale proves.

"We used 'Too Much of a Good Thing.' It is the best thing out."—*Dramatic Club, Fairview, Pa.*

IS THE EDITOR IN ?

A lively farce, by T. S. Denison; 4 m., 2 f. Time, 20 m. *Scene:* Country printing office. Brassy editor, poetical old maid, aggrieved subscribers. Very amusing; illustrates the trials of country journalism, and of country subscribers.

AN ONLY DAUGHTER.

A drama in 3 acts, by T. S. Denison; 5 m., 2 f. (and little girl) Time, 1 h., 15 m. *Scenes:* Handsome parlor, poorly furnished room. Old man, Yankee comedian leading lady, soubrette, worthless husband. This drama is full of touching pathos, but contains scenes of rich humor. Edith Harvey rejects a worthy suitor for an adventurer, with the usual results, intemperance abuse, desertion. Reconciliation and reform close the play. Nick Boone, the comedian, and Edith, the suffering wife, are very strong character

"Have played 'Only Daughter' to a very large audience with grand success."—*Secretary Dramatic Club, Botkins, O.*

WIDE ENOUGH FOR TWO.

A roaring farce, one of Denison's very best; 5 m., 2 f. Time, 45 m. Contains a rattling Dutch comedian. sharp Negro ditto, male crank, female literary crank, practical business man, and equally practical daughter. *Scene:* Plainly furnished room, no change. It is full of *busi ness* from beginning to end, and never fails to take. Mr Wickerwork's "schemes" are exceedingly ludicrous when put in operation. Fritz Kellar's predicament is fairly side splitting, but he finally turns the tables.

' One of the best farces in existence."—*Dramatic Club, Danville, Ind.*

A FAMILY STRIKE.

A farce in 1 act by T. S. Denison; 3 m., 3 f. Time, 20 m. *Scene:* Plain room Suggested by the great strikes of 1877; it illustrates strikes in the family in a very comical way. Mr. Blitzen, a very irascible old gentleman, his sentimental daughter Julia, his fashionable wife, and Mr. Gus Gullivant are the chief characters in a family misunderstanding. Gus is taken for somebody else, but all terminates happily when the mistakes are cleared.

THE MISSES BEERS.

A highly comical farce, by Emil Ludekens; 3 m., 3 f, Time, 25 m. The ludicrous features of this capital little farce depend upon the likeness existing between three ladies by the unromantic name of Beers of different families. The way their lovers get things mixed is keenly enjoyable. It is refined and telling humor. *Characters:* Two young couples, widow and widower.

ON GUARD

A farce, by C. F. Townsend; 4 m., 2 f. Time, 25 m. Full of *go*. Ludicrous situations. McFinnegan is a rare Irishman.

WHICH WILL HE MARRY ?

A farce in 1 act, by Thos E. Wilks; 2 m., 8 f. Time 20 m. *Scenes:* Interior. Richard Wiggs, a barber; hears that a young lady of his neighborhood has fallen heir to seven hundred pounds. Uncertain who the fortunate damsel i he determines to make love to all the young ladies of his acquaintance; u fortunately he commits himself in his zeal and the tempest raised among the squad of fiancees is ludicrous in the extreme. By a little adroit complimenting he succeeds in getting out of a very bad box.

MIKE DONOVAN'S COURTSHIP.

A comedietta in 2 acts; 1 m , 3 f. Time, 15 m. *Scenes:* Plain rooms. One darky female. Mike in one scene disguises as a gipsy fortune teller. Mike enlists in the army for three months. On his return he finds his sweetheart Hattie, engaged to another man. Under the guise of a fortune teller he works on her feelings until he regains her favor. A first-rate piece for a "chink" in a program.

A DESPERATE SITUATION; OR IN FOR A HOLIDAY.

A farce, by F. C. Burnand; 2 m., 3 f. Time, 25 m, *Scene:* Neatly furnished lodgings of a bachelor. Full of business and fun. Popple is :- love with Mrs. Waggles, a young widow. He is hard up and lacks the funds necessary to tak. her on a holiday excursion. By mistake a costly bonnet is delivered . P. Mrs. W is suspicious, thinks he is false, and a scene ensues. A happy thought suggests his pawning the bonnet which belongs to Mrs. O'Bobster. She traces it to P.'s lodgings and while there seeking it, Mr O'B., who is very jealous, happens in. Ludicrous denoument and explanations.

MY WIFE'S RELATIONS.

A comedietta in 1 act, by Walter Gordon; 4 m., 6 f. Time, 1 h. *Scene:* Neatly furnished room. There is a vein of humor pervading it, which, with the droll situations, make it highly enjoyable. A young husband finds himself seriously plagued by his wife's relatives. When things are no longer endurable the lucky arrival of the husband's sister, who pretends to be a cousin, makes herself at home, and borrows money, opens the wife's eyes to the unwarrantable liberties of her own relatives.

A WONDERFUL LETTER

A farce by C. F. Townsend; 4 m., 1 f. Time, 25 m. Very popular. Skipper is immensely funny. Easy of presentation.

I'M NOT MESILF AT ALL.

A farce by C A. Maltby; 3 m., 2 f. Time, 25 m. *Scene:* Breakfast-room in English villa. Old man, English cavalry captain, Phelim O'Rourke who palms himself off as an expected Mr. Hogan (he is a genuine son of the ould sod), Laura, the young lady of the house, chambermaid. Easily presented, and good where a *short* piece is wanted.

UNCLE DICK'S MISTAKE

A farce, by E. C. Whalen; 3 m., 2 f. Time, 20 m. The *mistake* was in proposing to the wrong woman. How Sammy, the enfant terrible, got Uncle Dick into the mistake, and how said uncle got out, will surely please.

A KISS IN THE DARK.

A farce, by J. B. Buckstone; 2 m., 3 :. Time, 30 m. *Scene:* A parlor. This play is very easily presented and takes well. Mr. Pettibone, who is lately married, fears that his wife may not love him. He asks his newly arrived friend, Frank Fathom, who was an old lover of hers, to test her fidelity. She overhears, and her willingness to flirt surprises both gentlemen. P. in a rage. He contrives to get ink on her nose and puts out the lights as if by accident. F. kisses Mrs P. and afterward the servant, spreading the ink considerably. Mrs. F. arrives. Very funny termination.

A BAD JOB.

A very ludicrous farce, by H. Elliott McBride; 3 m., 2 f. Time, 30 m. A tragedy man, a poetical man. a simple minded youth, fond of pie and anxious to marry, a fickle young lady and a widow. A taking piece, if rendered by those who properly appreciate the ludicrous.

PLAYED AND LOST.

A comedietta, by H. E. McBride; 3 m., 2 f. Time, 15 m. Good for a school entertainment. Two Yankee dialect parts. Takes off the modern flirt, and contains an excellent lesson.

BUMBLE'S COURTSHIP.

A capital dialogue; 1 m., 1 f. Time, 10 m. *Scenes:* Interior. Costume of beadle semi-military. This little sketch never fails to take. It represents the celebrated courtship of Beadle Bumble in Dickens' Oliver Twist. Nothing better can be found for a parlor or other light entertainment.

LUCY'S OLD MAN.

A sketch by H. E. McBride; 2 m., 3 f. Time, 10 m. Two mothers plan for their children to marry. Erastus visits the young lady in the disguise of an old man seeking charity, but gets none from the fair Eleanor. The kindhearted cousin Lucy wins the prize unwittingly.

IN THE WRONG HOUSE. (TWO T. J's.)

A farce, by Martin Becher; 4 m., 2 f. Time, 30 m. *Scene:* A plain room. Two light comedians, and two excellent parts for ladies. An eccentric author hires the lodgings of a young man in his absence; the latter has eloped with a young lady, and an irate father is in pursuit with a detective. All confront the author about the same time, to the complete mystification of everybody. Very laughable throughout. A fine parlor play.

MY JEREMIAH.

A very amusing farce, by H. E. McBride; 3 m., 2 f. Time, 20 m. Irate female seeking her hen-pecked "old man." One male darky, two Yankee characters.

THE COW THAT KICKED CHICAGO.

A humorous farce, by H. E. McBride; 3 m., 2 f. Time, 20 m. Very funny An Irishman, an Irishwoman, a Dutchman and a Yankee, each advance various theories as to the cause of the Chicago fire to Mrs. Pinkerton, a curiosity seeker.

THE BABES IN THE WOOD.

A ludicrous farce, based on the story of the babes in the wood; 4 m., 3 f. Time, 25 m. *Scenes:* Interior and a wood Costumes may be made easily and cheaply. Two overgrown persons for the "babes" make the piece a great success.

BARDELL VS. PICKWICK.

A farce; 6 m. (with attorneys, crier, etc.), 2 f. Time, 25 m. *Scene:* A court room. This play is arranged from the immortal Pickwick Papers of Charles Dickens. It is exceedingly humorous in every detail. It gives an excellent chance to " take off " local celebrities.

THE WOMEN OF LOWENBURG.

A historical comedy in five scenes, by E. Murray; numerous males and females, according to material (not less than 10 of each). Time, 30 m. *Scene:* The town hall of Lowenburg, Germany, during the thirty years' war. This is a most excellent piece for school exhibitions and literary societies, where there are plenty of actors. The men of Lowenburg attempted to compel the women to change their religion as the men themselves had already done. The town council passed a decree to that effect, but the women repair in a body to the town hall to protest. The men hastily decamp in ludicrous fear at the approach of their spouses. A vein of delicious humor runs through the whole.

IN THE DARK.

A society farce, by W. G. Van T. Sutphen; 4 m., 2 f. Time, 20 minutes. Two society young men call upon an aristocratic family, where there is a beautiful young heiress and a maiden lady of uncertain years, with the same surname, which leads to amusing complications. Both the gentlemen are fortune hunters. When pressed to stay for dinner, one discovers that he is not in full dress. He hits on the device of borrowing the other's coat to go into dinner. Number two, tired of waiting, borrows the coat of the butler, and follows to the dining room. Things get badly mixed, and just then the gas goes out. A splendid piece for light comedy purposes.

HOMŒOPATHY; Or the Family Cure.

A farce by J. C. Frank; 5 m., 3 f. Time, 30 m. *Scenes:* Chamber and street. *Characters:* A grasping old deacon with matrimonial designs on a charming young lady; Pat, the Irish doctor, who aids the favored lover to circumvent the deacon; indignant parent; widow with matrimonial designs. May introduce fine Irish songs. A very taking Irish play, comical, but refined.

SQUEERS' SCHOOL.

A sketch from Nicholas Nickleby, by Charles Dickens; 4 m (and school boys), 2 f. Time, 10 m. *Scene:* A schoolroom. This is a scene in which the brutal Squeers attempts to chastise poor Smike, and is himself soundly punished by Nicholas Nickleby.

THE FATHER OF HIS COUNTRY.

By Marion West. An excellent entertainment, not only for Washington's Birthday but for any Friday afternoon in school. It contains a brief examination of the events of his life, eloquent extracts from Webster, Brougham and others suitable for speaking, and several *tableaux* illustrating points in his great career. Singing of patriotic airs. Time, 30 m.

WHO SHALL BE QUEEN OF MAY?

A beautiful little piece by Marion Wayland, suitable for not only May Day, but for any time in summer when flowers are plenty and light dresses may be worn. 1 m., 5 f., fairies. etc. Time, 30 m.

DAY BEFORE CHRISTMAS.

By Alice P. Carter, a rollicking, jolly, old-time piece of Christmas fun, songs, Christmas gifts, fairy dances, etc. 4 m., 2 f., fairies, etc. Time, 20 m.

THE CHRISTMAS SHIP.

A sparkling little musical play by Nettie H. Pelham; 4 m. 3 f. Time, 20 m. Can be played in any schoolroom or parlor. By omitting Santa Claus and naming the piece, " When My Ship Comes In," it is a pretty piece for any time of year. The music is all popular, such as any person who sings at all knows by heart.

WOOING UNDER DIFFICULTIES.

A farce, by John T. Douglass, 4 m., 3 f. *Scenes:* Interior. Time, 35 m. Mr. and Mrs. Jill expect Mr. St. Pauls who is intended for their daughter. At the same time a new man-servant, Henry, is expected. Henry, who is a good looking fellow, is mistaken for Mr. St. Pauls, and is asked out to walk with them. Meanwhile Mr. St. Pauls puts in an appearance and is put to servant's work. This piece is very easily presented, and the ludicrous situations make it uproariously funny.

A MODEL OF A WIFE.

A farce, by Alfred Wigan, 3 m., 2 f. Time, 25 m. Bonnefoi has lodgings opposite Stump's studio. He falls in love with Clara, the cousin of Mrs. S. He calls and leaves note which falls into the hands of Mrs. S. Stump is very jealous and makes a scene. The Frenchman calls later in despair, and threatens to blow his brains out because Tom, the office boy, leads him to believe he has been making love to a dummy. Tom places Clara in a chair veiled as a lay figure, and B. goes through ridiculous scene apostrophizing "Ze beautiful figair." Good piece for light entertainments.

LOVE AND RAIN.

An interlude; 1 m., 1 f. Time, 20 m. Lady Desmond is shut up in the country during a spell of very wet weather. She invites a stranger to take temporary shelter during a heavy shower. She first thinks him a glazier, then is terribly alarmed lest he is a noted robber, finally discovers him to be a person whom she greatly wished to meet. Very entertaining, ending in a match.

TWENTY MINUTES UNDER AN UMBRELLA.

A sketch by A. W. Dubourg; 1 m., 1 f. Time, 20 m. This is a very interesting little his-tory of what happened to Cousin Frank and Cousin Kate, while a timely shower compelled them to spend twenty minutes under an umbrella.

JUST MY LUCK.

A farce, by Alfred Maltby; 4 m., 3 f. Time, 20 m. *Scene:* Plain room. Capt. Dunn, a humbug, comes to woo Letitia Crumpets, but is arrested for debt to the disgust of the young lady. Mr. Crumpets goes swimming, fishermen steal his clothes, and leave theirs. C. is obliged to return in fisherman garb. Is mistaken by Capt. Dunn for burglar; amusing skirmish. Mrs. C. intercepts a note signed "M. C." and thinks her husband is engaged in a flirtation. Mike, who wrote the note to the servant, mistakes C. for a rival. They fight. Re-enter Dunn and policeman, general scuffle, mesmeric business, very funny. Place for good song.

A LUCKY SIXPENCE.

A farce, by E. J. Browne; 4 m., 2 f. Time, 30 m. Mr. Heartyman expects his nephew, Charles, from foreign parts. Scampwell, a genteel adventurer, hard up, overhears the old gen-tleman and his daughter Julia talking in the garden about Charles. He concludes to pass for Charles, hoping to "raise the wind." When the real Charles arrives things become exceedingly interesting, and he is denounced as bogus. He finally proves his identity by means of a lucky sixpence. Every part good, Starcher, the governess, and Scamp in particular.

A SILENT WOMAN.

A farce, by T. H. Lacy; 2 m., 1 f. Time, 25 m. Arthur Merton is engaged to Marianne Sandford. He travels extensively, and his knowledge of the world changes his views materially concerning women. He longs for one who is not loquacious. He reveals his feelings to Mr. S. who enters into a clever little conspiracy whereby the daughter plays deaf and dumb. Arthur is delighted, and when he discovers the ruse, is willing to forgive the fair deceiver. A capital piece for parlor performance.

THAT RASCAL PAT.

A rattling farce, by J. Holmes Grover; 3 m., 2 f. Time, 35 m. *Scene:* Public room in a hotel. This is the very cream of Irish farce. The wrath of Major Puffjacket in contrast with the inimitable drollery of Pat McNoggerty must be seen to be appreciated. It brings down the house, especially when Pat tries to serve two masters at once. Clubs will not miss it if they try this piece.

CUT OFF WITH A SHILLING.

A comedietta in one act, by S. Theyre Smith; 2 m., 1 f. Time, 25m. Sam Gaythorne marries Kittie without his uncle's consent. Uncle cuts him off with a shilling, and sends coin by mail. Col. Berners, the uncle, happens to call by accident, and, not knowing K., begins to draw out her history. The way she wins over the irascible old chap is very taking. This play will surely please.

PLAYS FOR MALE CHARACTERS.

TAMING A TIGER.

A farce; 3 m. Time, 20 m. A roaring piece of fun from beginning to end. The best kind of after-piece, or good to fill in when there are plenty of males. Sure to take.

A VERY PLEASANT EVENING.

A farce, by W. E. Suter; 3 m. Time, 30 m. This farce is the very quintescence of the ludicrous. Mr. Tremor goes out with his daughter. Breamer slips in hoping to meet Mary Anne, the maid. Screamer also slips in to see Betsey, another servant. He carefully locks door after him. Each hears the other and is frightened. Soon Mr. T. comes back, and the various dodges of the three as they try to get rid of one another, are simply *immense*.

THE FRIENDLY MOVE.

A sketch from Our Mutual Friend, by Charles Dickens; 4 males. Time, 20 m. This piece represents the consummate rascality of old Silas Wegg in his scheme to defraud Mr. Boffin. The ex-ballad seller, who "declined and fell," is sure to draw. Amusing.

INITIATING A GRANGER.

A roaring farce, by T. S. Denison; 10 m. Time, 25 m. Full of practical jokes. *Scene:* A student's room. This farce has had a large and steady sale. Though the "Granger" fever is no more, the humor of this farce will always amuse.
"It was laughable beyond description."—*J. W. Simmons, Lawrence, Mich.*

COUNTRY JUSTICE.

A very amusing country lawsuit, by T. S. Denison; 8 m. (may admit further a jury of 6 or 12.) Time, 15 m. This little play will do equally well for boys or full grown men. The testimony, the arguments and the verdict are all remarkable. It is always popular.

THE MOVEMENT CURE.

Very funny scene in a doctor's office; 5 m.. (may make principal, negroes if desired.) Time, 10 m. The office boys conclude to try the movement cure on a patient, and "thump" him more than is agreeable to the invalid. Very amusing diagnosis of the case.

TWO GENTLEMEN IN A FIX.

Capital little farce by W. E. Suter; 2 m. Time, 15 m. *Scene:* A railroad depot. The gentlemen impede each other in the doorway with their luggage, and in the wrangle both miss the train. They enter into an animated and highly amusing discussion which ends in the discovery that the younger is the prospective son-in-law of the elder. When the discussion is ended they both stick in the door and miss the next train.

I'LL STAY AWHILE.

A humorous farce, by H. E. McBride; 4 m. Time, 20 m. An old widower disappointed in love and politics becomes a hypochondriac and determines he must die. A device on the part of his friends causes him to think it best to stay awhile. One good Irish character

THE CIRCUMLOCUTION OFFICE.

Arranged from Charles Dickens' story of Little Dorrit; 6 males required, may admit 10. Time, 15 m. *Scenes:* Offices. A splendid illustration of red tape as applied in the British government offices. Very humorous.

PLAYS FOR FEMALE CHARACTERS.

THE PULL BACK.

A laughable farce by T. S. Denison; 6 f. Time, 20 m. *Scene:* Waiting room of depot. Plain room will answer. This little play is very popular. Excellent old-fashioned old lady character, and her adventures among the devotees of fashion.
"I used the Pull Back in my school. It took splendidly."—*Anna E. Musgrove, Metropolis, Ill.*

TWO GHOSTS IN WHITE.

A humorous farce, by T. S. Denison; boarding school life; 8 f. Time, 20 m. Very funny throughout, and contains some excellent hits. The ghosts result from an innocent freak of the girls which terminates in a ludicrous scene. Severe lady principal, gushing lady patron, Irish servant, jolly girls.

PETS OF SOCIETY.

A farce, by T. S. Denison; 7 f. Time, 23 m. *Scene:* Handsome parlors. German or Scandinavian girl, Irish girl, female dudes. Takes off the fashionable girl of the period to a dot. The conversation and the incidents are ludicrous in the extreme.
"It must be read to be appreciated."—*Theatrical Record.*

MRS. GAMP'S TEA.

Arranged from Dickens' novel, Martin Chuzzlewit; 2 f. Mrs. Gamp and Betsy Prig. Time, 10 m. Those who are familiar with the novel will need no description of these characters. An amusing quarrel arises over Mrs. Gamp's invisible friend, Mrs. Harris.

A FAIR ENCOUNTER.

A very lively comedietta, by Charles Marsham Rae; 2 f. Time, 25 m. A splendid case of diamond cut diamond. Just the thing for two bright ladies.

MITSU-YU NISSI, Or the Japanese Wedding.

A play of Japanese life, in 3 acts; 6 m., 6 f., servants, etc. Time, 1 h., 15 m. The costumes and furnishing wholly Japanese, after the style of the mikado. May be prepared at home very easily, with small expense. *Scenes:* Interior of Japanese house, and the interior of a small Buddhist Temple. A striking, novel and popular entertainment Specially suitable for church societies. *Full directions for performance.*

TEMPERANCE PLAYS.

THE SPARKLING CUP.

A temperance play in 5 acts, by T. S. Denison; 12 m., 4 f. Time, 2 h. *Scenes:* Handsome parlor, counting house, saloon, street, reading room. May be produced in any hall. *Characters:* Old man, drunkard, canting hypocrite, villain, Yankee comedian, German ditto, women of the temperance union, temperance lecturer, loafers, little girl, etc. A thrilling play which always takes. It contains a very pathetic song by the little beggar girl.
"The Sparkling Cup met with great success. It is the great rival of Ten Nights in a Bar Room."—*W. F. Kuhn, DeGraff, O.*

ON THE BRINK; Or the Reclaimed Husband.

A temperance play in 2 acts, by H. Elliott McBride; 12 m., 3 f. Time, 2 h. *Scenes:* Neatly furnished rooms, poor room, a barroom. Yankee comedian, old bachelor in search of a wife, old maid in search of a husband, the victims of drink, a disappointed politician, the insane wife. Seven of the male characters have short parts. This play always takes; combines racy humor with tender pathos. The part of the insane wife, is very touching.
"We rendered On the Brink a number of times very successfully to crowded houses."—*Dramatic Club, Cordova, Minn.*

FRUITS OF THE WINE CUP.

A temperance play in 3 acts, by J. H. Aller; 6 m., 4 f. Time; 1 hour. *Scenes:* Handsome dining room, plain sitting rooms, and a street. *Characters:* A rich merchant who is ruined by drink, his lovely daughter Kate Andrews, her would-be suitor, who is a forger and villain, Speculation, the roving ne'er-do-well, who unearths all Andrews' plans, etc. Always popular with temperance societies, contains some thrilling scenes. It is very easily presented.

HARD CIDER.

An amusing little sketch, by T. S. Denison; 4 m., 2 f. Time, 10 m. Just the thing for a short entertainment anywhere, in school, parlor, or Red Ribbon Club.

TEN NIGHTS IN A BAR ROOM.

A temperance play in 5 acts, from T. S. Arthur's story of the same name; 7 m., 4 f. Time, 2 h. *Scenes:* Interior and exterior of the "Sickle and Sheaf;" a landscape, a wood, a poor room in the house of Morgan, the drunkard. Contains a strong list of characters representing nearly all classes of society. Switchel is a fine Yankee comedian. Ten nights in a Bar Room has been presented thousands of times, and is always a success when justice is done the parts. Can be presented in any hall.

OUT IN THE STREETS.

A temperance play in 3 acts, by S. N. Cook; 6 m., 4 f. Time, 1 h., 15 m. A celebrated play, and one that will always take. The trials of Mrs. Bradford are very touching. The Darky, North Carolina Pete, is very funny.

DENISON'S POPULAR OPERETTAS.

BONNYBELL: Or, Cinderella's Cousin.

A musical play for young folks and children; libretto by Emma C. Vogelgesang, music by W. G. Farrar. Seven principal characters, knights, ladies, attendants, etc., *ad lib.* Time required about 1 h. *Scenes:* The home of Bonnybell and a hall in the castle of the Prince. This little play is so simple that it may be presented in any schoolroom or parlor.
"It abounds in pleasing, tripping songs, cheerful dialogue, a commendable plot, and attractive music."—*Inter-Ocean.*
"Was produced here and met with decided approval."—*E. Grantz, Spring Valley, Minn., N. Y.*
Price, 25 Cents.

ELMA, THE FAIRY CHILD.

By Frances M. Payson. A delightful play by a popular writer of music. Elma, the mortal, longs to be something different, and has her wish gratified in suddenly becoming a fairy. She makes the acquaintance of the fairy queen, Puck, and other notabilities of that wonderful land of flowers and melody. The piece sparkles from beginning to end with pretty rhymes and choice music. Time required about 1 h. 30 m. Five principal characters, male and female; others to fill up. The play opens at Elma's home, but the scene is soon transferred to fairyland; admits of beautiful effects in the way of fairy costumes (which may be made at home) artificial and natural flowers, etc.
"Pretty and easily managed, being quite simple, and capable of being costumed and acted by any company."—*Springfield (Mass.) Republican.*
Price, 25 Cents.

POCAHONTAS.

A musical burlesque in 2 acts, by Welland Hendrick. Introduces Pocahontas, John Smith, John Rolfe, Mahogany, a gentleman of ebony finish, braves, etc.; 2 females, Pocahontas, and Ann Eliza Brown. Time, 1 h. The old story of Pocahontas is here done over in most laughable fashion. The dialogue is very funny throughout. The songs are adapted to popular airs, so that presentation will be very easy. The excessive dignity of the Indian chief in contrast with the antics of Mahogany, and the dilemma of John Smith, when Ann Eliza Brown appears, can scarcely fail to convulse any aud'
Price, 15 Cents.

THE STAR DRAMA.

Price 15 Cents Each, Postpaid.

This series includes only plays of the highest order of merit. They are rich in variety of incident and spirited in action. The dramas combine tender pathos, delightful humor, and sparkling wit. The farces are brimful of the rarest fun. This series is very carefully revised by an experienced editor. Each play is unabridged. They are unequaled in fullness of stage directions typography and print. There are no obsolete or worthless plays in this list, and nothing in any way *objectionable.* These plays are more difficult than those given under "Amateur Plays," still any good amateur club can present anything here. In this catalogue when costumes are not mentioned there is nothing out of the ordinary line of dress or "costumes of the day."

LOUVA, THE PAUPER.

A play in 5 acts, by T. S. Denison; 9 m., 4 f. Time, 2 h. *Scenes:* Room in log house, room in planter's house, hut in mountains. *Characters:* Yankee comedian, darky ditto, a specimen of Southern "poor white trash," villain, Louva (the heroine), Southern planter, gipsy crone, darky crone, etc. Storm scene. This is one of the best plays for amateurs ever written, if popularity is a test of merit. It is intensely interesting and pathetic. It admits of striking scenic effects. Act I, Louva's tyrants. Act II, freedom promised and denied. Act III, the trial. Act IV, the flight. Act V, pursuit; death in the mountains; retribution.

"Send sample copy of a play that is as good as Louva, the Pauper. That took splendidly here."
—*G. J. Railsbach, Minier, Ill., Dramatic Club.*

UNDER THE LAURELS.

A play in 5 acts, by T. S. Denison; 5 m., 4 f. *Scenes:* A handsome parlor, deserted cabin in mountains, log jail. *Characters:* Mrs. Milford, elderly lady; Rose, her adopted daughter, plays a very spirited part; designing middle-aged man, who tries to win Rose; Frank, the accepted lover, who is the victim of conspiracy; Darky comedian; Yankee ditto; soubrette, etc. Not a poor character in the play. A thrilling scene at cabin; fine storm scene. *Place:* Mountains of the Central South. Under the Laurels rivals "Louva" and though not having the touching pathos of that play it excels it in *business* and variety of humor and action. Act I. Conspiracy. Act II. The Lost Inheritance. Act III. The haunted cabin, the storm in the mountains, Cliffville jail, the regulators. Act IV. Despair. Act V. Escape, capture, rescue. All's well.

"We rendered 'Under the Laurels' to a large and critical audience, with telling effect. It is a capital play, and we shall try more of your plays."—*Dramatic Club, Danville, Ind.*

"Under the Laurels gave splendid satisfaction."—*I. R. Stevens, Manager Dramatic Club, Cantril, Ia.*

A SOLDIER OF FORTUNE.

A comedy drama in 5 acts, by Warren J. Brier; 8 m., 3 f. Time, 2 h., 30 m. *Scenes:* Handsomely furnished parlor, library, doctor's office, a wood; fine opportunities for stage setting. *Characters:* Middle-aged gentleman, Spanish-American villain, Irishman, Darky comedian, juvenile comedian, old man, old maid, society young ladies, etc. Dramatic clubs can find nothing better than this play. It always takes. Its humor is rich and abundant. It affords ample scope for good acting.

"We are well pleased with 'A Soldier of Fortune.' Do not think we have had a better play."
—*W. H. Stewart, Sec. Dramatic Club, Le Sueur, Minn.*

A REGULAR FIX.

A farce, by J. M. Morton; 6 m., 4 f. Time, 40 m. *Scene:* Elegant parlor. As its name indi·cates this farce gets things in a *regular* fix. Hugh de Brass by mistake, gets into the wrong house very early in the morning, just after a grand ball; goes to sleep in an arm chair; wakes, overhears family secrets, is taken for somebody else, etc. His ingenious efforts to baffle inquiry, and his knowledge of the secrets of others keep up a torrent of continuous fun. The late Mr. Sothern deemed the character of DeBrass worthy his efforts.

THE YANKEE DETECTIVE.

A stirring drama in 3 acts, by W. E. Stedman; 8 m., 3 f. Time, 2 h. *Scenes:* Detective offices, saloon, hotel at Long Branch, deserted laborers' quarters at a wild spot on the coast. *Leading Characters:* "The Yankee Detective," who assumes in turn role of plain citizen, traveling musician, summer resort boarder, and German sausage vender. This role affords fine opportunities for character representation. Typical villain, and gang of counterfeiters. "Ole Tennessee Sam" is a first-class darky comedy character. Mrs. Willoughby, rich widow, Lulu Southard, the wronged wife, and Granny Wizzle, housekeeper for the gang. This play is very strong in rapidity of movement, variety of incident, scenic effects, and the culminating danger of the detective when he is captured by the gang of counterfeiters.

"There is a general request that we play it again."—*Sons of Veterans, Carson, Ia.*

THE PET OF PARSONS' RANCH.

A comedy-drama of Western life, by W. F. Felch; 9 m., 2 f. Time, 2 h. *Scenes*: Interior at Parsons' hotel in the Sierras, and exterior in the stage robbery on the " Divide." Leading man, a "crack" stage driver of the gold-hunting days. Neil Norris, a gambler and "road agent," Old Pap Reeder, with his gold-extraction process, Aaron Parsons, a hunted man, miners, travelers, etc. Leading lady, Pet Parsons, (comedy) a real specimen of Rocky Mountain womanhood. Several characters afford fine opportunities to the ambitious amateur of the best grade. This is a wholesome sympathetic play that is brim full of the bracing air of its location—the Sierras of California before the days of railroads.

THE DANGER SIGNAL.

A drama in 2 acts, by T. S. Denison: 7 m , 4 f. Time, 2 h. *Scene:* A plain room, no change. *Costumes*: Every-day dress. *Place*: A lonely island in the "Great Lakes." Very easily presented. In this respect the amateur's *best*. No weak characters. Leading man, middle aged (very strong), Irish and Darky comedians, Irish maid-of-all work, old lady (excellent), young heroine, young lady with more money than brains, a quack doctor full of theories, a United States engineer, a sentimental young (silly old) bachelor. This play is one of Denison's very best. The plot hinges on the central idea of Enfield's wrongs, and his burning desire for revenge which takes possession of him with the subordinate idea of concealing Stella's identity. Spirited action. The Danger Signal is certainly equal to Louva and Under the Laurels, these three leading in sale all others by the same author.

" It is without doubt one of the very best plays on the modern stage. Its humor is rich and abundant; its pathos touching, yet highly interesting."—*Dramatic Club, Wyanet, Ill.*

CASTE.

A comedy in 3 acts, by T. W. Robertson; 5 m., 3 f. Time, 2 h., 30 m. *Scenes*: Plain room, fashionable lodgings. Light comedian, eccentric old comedian young Englishman, leading lady, young lady, a Marquise. Costumes of the day (two military). Capt. D'Alroy, son of a Marquise, in defiance of *caste*, marries a young actress, and finds himself burdened with a drunken old father-in-law; D'Alroy goes as a soldier to India, and his wife suffers want in his absence. He returns, and is reconciled to his haughty mother. This play has been presented again and again for years in Europe and America. Every character is good. Eccles (old man) is particularly strong; he and Sam Gerridge furnish abundant humor.

NOT SUCH A FOOL AS HE LOOKS.

A farcical drama in 3 acts, by H. J. Byron; 5 m., 3 f. Time, 2 h. *Scenes*: Handsome drawing-rooms, plain room. *Characters*: A simple-minded baronet (who proves to be no baronet), a money broker, shabby middle-aged lawyer's clerk, (low English comedian middle-aged lady, young lady, designing old female, etc. Byron's plays are always good, and this is one of his best. It abounds in telling situations, and has genuine humor. The plot is ingenious; the chief interest depending on the discovering who Sir Simon Simple really is. Mr Mold and Mrs. Mold, who " 'opes as 'ow she doesn't intrude," are taking comedy characters.

HOME.

A comedy in 3 acts by T. W. Robertson; 4 m., 3 f. Time, 2 h. *Scene*: Handsome parlor, no change. Two light comedians, old man, servants, designing lady, two charming young ladies. Young Dorrison (alias Col. White), has been in America for several years, and returns to find Mrs. Pinchbeck, an adventuress, about to entrap his unsuspecting father into a matrimonial alliance, at the instigation of her gambling brother. White, concealing his identity, determines to save his father, and engages in a flirtation with Mrs. P. to that end. The elder Dorrison detects White, and in a rage at the perfidy of his guest, orders him from the house. White, who has fallen in love with Dora Thornhough, discovers himself The noble conduct of Mrs. P., really the victim of her brother, brings the play to a capital climax.

THE ROUGH DIAMOND, (The Country Cousin.)

A farce, by J. B. Buckstone; 4 m , 3 f. Time, 40 m. *Scene*: Drawing-room. This is one of the best farces before the public. The best actors of the day have appeared in it. Margery, the "Rough Diamond," a beautiful country lass, marries Sir William Evergreen. Her Cousin ᵓe comes to see her. Their talk about the pigs, the neighbors, etc , and their actions are extremely ludicrous to Sir W. and his fashionable friends. But circumstances illustrate well the sterling qualities of the Rough Diamond, compared with that of the fashionable Lady Plato. This farce is exceedingly funny, easily produced, and has an excellent moral.

THE PERSECUTED DUTCHMAN.

A farce, by S. Barry; 6 m., 3 f. Time, 35m. *Scene*: A hotel. Dutch and Irish comedians, sentimental young lady, dude, This farce is one of which the public never tires. Joh ɪ Schmidt, the persecuted Dutchman, is a commercial traveler at a hotel. Elopement of the sentimental young lady with a "nice" young man; wrathful rival, irate parent. Dutchy is mistaken for the "villain." No end of fun. The situations are indescribably ludicrous.

THE LIMERICK BOY; Or Paddy's Mischief.

A capital Irish farce, by James Pilgrim; 5 m , 2 f. Time, 30 m. *Scenes*: Plain rooms (may have street view) Paddy Miles, always full of mischief; Dr. Coates, the subject of one of Paddy's jokes; Mrs. Fidget; Jane, her daughter; Harry, son of Doctor; Job, a gardener. This little farce has the genuine ring of Irish humor

THE TOODLES.

A drama in 2 acts; 6 m. (and 3 farmers with a few lines each), 2 f. Time, 1 h., 15 m. *Scenes*: Landscape, plain chamber, churchyard; (may be easily presented with scenes all interior.) Toodles, comedian, is incomparable. Mrs. Toodles also has an excellent comedy part. George Acorn and Frank are brothers. Frank wins the girl to whose hand George aspired. Latter goes to sea, and returns after twenty years; finds his niece engaged to a young sailor; revenge is in his heart, and he determines to drive his brother's family out of the old homestead under the terms of his father's will. Mary's trials and pleadings at last soften his heart. This play will win the sympathies of any audience.

MY TURN NEXT.

A capital farce, by Thos. J. Williams; 4 m., 3 f. Time, 45 m. *Scene*: A parlor. Mr. Twitters, a very timid apothecary, has just married a widow. Her former husband, who was constantly dodging debtors, had assumed various names, and Twitters is horrified to hear people speak of his wife, as Mrs. Green, Brown, Black, etc., successively. Peggy, the servant, hints mysteriously that Mrs T. made way with them. Twitters is greatly alarmed, fears he may meet the same fate. He starts when his wife whets the carving knife, fears poison, suspects the ale. Tim, his assistant, is sure *he* has been poisoned, and the fear of the two is excruciatingly ludicrous. Peggy is a capital soubrette.

TURN HIM OUT.

A farce, by T. J. Williams; 3 m., 2 f. Time, 35 m. *Scene*: A parlor. *Characters*: Leading lady, good comic soubrette, male exquisite, comedian, etc. This farce, like all of Williams' plays, is first-class. Roseleaf calls at the house of Moke, and making himself disagreeable to Mrs. M., Susan, the maid, asks her lover, Nobbs, to "turn him out." Moke meantime appears and Nobbs puts him out by mistake. Roseleaf meantime is concealed. He reappears and so does Moke. They form an alliance to pitch Nobbs out but it fails ingloriously, and Moke goes out a second time Enraged, he again appears in *disguise*, and by a strange turn of affairs is carried off in a chest.

LARKINS' LOVE LETTERS.

A farce, by T. J. Williams; 3 m., 2 f. Time, 45 m. *Scene*: Plain room. Every character good. Pompous and irascible ex-colonel, two excellent comedians, leading lady, soubrette. There is no *love* at all in this play. The fun lies in the attempt of Boyleover and Lynx to discover the missing letters. In their zeal they turn the apartments of Mr. Benjamin Bobbins upside down. Easy to present, and full of *business*.

ICI ON PARLE FRANCAIS.

A farce, by T. J. Williams; 3 m., 4 f. Time, 40 m. *Scenes*: Apartments in a lodging house. Good Frenchman, excitable major and his young wife, Mr. and Mrs. Spriggins, Anna Maria (last three fine comedy.) Mr. Spriggins' "French before breakfast;" the wrath of the mistaken and jealous major, the comical attempts of the Frenchman to be polite under trying circumstances, all combine to make this one of the best of farces.

THE LADY OF LYONS; Or, Love and Pride.

By Sir Edward Bulwer Lytton. A romantic drama in 5 acts; 8 m., 4 f. (four other males with a few lines each). Time of representation, 3 h. *Period*: The French revolution. *Scene*: Lyons. *Costumes*: French of that day. Four of the male and three of the female characters are excellent. Many famous actors and actresses have appeared in this popular play, which is one of the best standard plays on the modern stage. It abounds in brilliant dialogue and stirring scenes. This edition is complete in every respect.

EAST LYNNE.

A drama in 5 acts, from the novel of the same name by Mrs. Henry Wood; 8 m., 6 f. Time, 2 h., 15 m. *Scenes*: Chambers and landscapes. This favorite play is so well known that little need be said of its merits. Different stars have played it throughout the Union. Lady Isabel, Cornelia and Mr. Carlyle are strong characters.

THE TICKET-OF-LEAVE MAN.

A drama in 4 acts, by Tom Taylor; 8 m., 3 f. Time, 2 h., 45m. *Place*: London. *Scenes*: Public houses, offices and plain rooms. *Characters*: Thieves; a detective; Bob Brierly, the unsuspecting country lad; bill broker; two young ladies; comedy lady. A first-class stock play, good at all times. The plot hinges on the fact that Bob Brierly is induced to pass counterfeit money by James Dalton, "the Tiger." Brierly is sent to Portland prison for four years, but by good behavior obtains a ticket-of-leave, and enters the employ of Mr. Gibson, the banker. Here he is discovered by Dalton and Moss, who, on his refusal to aid them in robbing the bank, denounce him to Gibson. He loses his place, and with his wife (May Edwards) is reduced to great distress. Brierly finally redeems himself by exposing their plan to break into the bank. This fine play sustains a thrilling interest. Green Jones and wife are oddly humorous.

WON AT LAST.

A comedy in 3 acts, by Wybert Reeve, 7 m., 3 f. Time, 1 h., 45 m. *Scenes*: Drawing room, office, street. *Characters*: Old man, low comedian, villain, leading lady, walking lady, soubrette. A clean cut play, with some very exciting business at the close of Act II in the bill broker's office, also at the denouement when the villain Buchanan is so unexpectedly led into the presence of officers summoned by himself to drag away his victim, Capt. Warburton. The minor comedy parts admirably light up the darker colors of the plot.

SOLON SHINGLE; Or, the People's Lawyer.

A comedy in 2 acts, by J. S. Jones; 7 m. (with males to form court and jury in trial scene), 2 f. Time, 1 h., 30 m. *Scenes:* Plain rooms, counting house, street, court room. This is one of the best comedies ever put on the stage. Solon Shingle will convulse the audience with his droll Yankee humor. This is practically the same piece that was played for years by Denman Thompson under the title of Joshua Whitcomb.

GRANDFATHER'S MISTAKE; Or, the Chimney Corner.

A domestic drama in 2 acts, by H. T. Craven; 5 m., 2 f. Time, 1 h., 30 m. *Scenes:* Interiors. Solomon Probity, the grandfather, has lost the proper use of his mental facultie through old age. Not aware of what he is doing he conceals a box containing a large sum o. money, the legacy of Grace Emery, in the chimney. When the money is missed a note is found in the drawer from John Probity, the grandson, informing his parents that he has fled, and asking them to forgive his rash act. He is at once suspected of having stolen the money, whereas he referred to his running away because of his hopeless love for Grace. A rival has him arrested, but all is explained by the sudden return of memory to Grandfather Probity. This is a very fascinating play.

LOST IN LONDON.

A drama in 3 acts; 6 m., and 3 f. Time, 1 h., 45 m. *Scenes:* Interiors, landscape and interior of coal mine. A touching and powerful play. John Armroyd, a miner, marries a beautiful young wife. She is enticed away from him by Gilbert Featherstone, but bitterly repents her folly. Armroyd follows her to London, and finds her while Featherstone is giving a party. Nellie Armroyd swoons, and is seized with a violent illness. Afterward she recovers just in time to prevent a deadly encounter between the two men, but dies in Job's arms. Two or three characters speak the broad North of England dialect. Job's grief and Nellie's repentance are very touching.

LONDON ASSURANCE.

A comedy in 5 acts, by Dion Boucicault; 9 m., 3 f. Time, about 2 h., 30 m. *Scenes:* Handsome interiors and lawn. "Assurance" is well represented in several of the characters, for surely there was never a more "cheeky" individual than Dazzle, or a more impertinent one than Meddle. Lady Gay Spanker is unique in her dashing character. Old Courtney is surpassed only by his son Charles in their notions of what constitute a gentleman of the day; in short, every character is a study, and good. It is a capital piece for strong clubs. Plenty of fun, nothing dragging. It sparkles from beginning to end.

A QUIET FAMILY

A farce, by William E. Suter; 4 m., 4 f. Time, 45 m. *Scenes:* Plain rooms. *Characters:* Two married couples and two couples of lovers (including two servants). A sprightly play. Two of the married couples are the victims of too much family government. The polite quarrels wich take place are absurd to the last degree. The servants follow the example of their superiors. The "downtrodden" finally conspire together for mutual relief with surprising and highly satisfactory results.

JOHN SMITH.

A farce, by W. Hancock; 5 m., 3 f. Time, 30 m. *Scene:* Plain room. Every character good. An exceedingly funny piece. Old Smith takes a room which by a strange coincidence has been taken by his runaway son and wife. Smith to his amazement finds letters awaiting him, a boy calls to measure him for boots, etc. He concludes to take a nap. While he is asleep young Smith and wife enter, and the former, who is an actor, commences to rehearse a tragic part to the terror of Old Smith and Tom who are concealed in the room. A ludicrous scene ends in reconciliation.

THE TWO PUDDIFOOTS.

A rattling farce, by J. M. Morton; 3 m., 3 f. Time, 40 m. *Scene:* Plain apartment. Buffles, in looking for a husband for his niece Caroline, concludes that Puddifoot Junior will do. Latter comes, but his father happens to arrive same day. Puddifoot Senior concludes for a joke he will woo Caroline himself. Passes for Puddifoot Junior. Latter turns th ables on him in a very unexpected way. And Mrs. Figsby, the housekeeper, discovers Puddifoot Senior to be an old flame of hers. Together they corner him. Characters all good, especially Buffles, Peggy and Puddifoots.

MY NEIGHBOR'S WIFE.

A farce, by Alfred Bunn; 3 m., 3 f. Time, 45 m. *Scene:* Plain room. Smith and Brown unknown to each other, attempt a flirtation with Mrs. Somerton, their neighbor's wife. She promptly tells her husband, by whose advice she allows each to come for a little supper at the same time. They are greatly annoyed with each other's society, and to their consternation the husband drops in; soon after their wives drop in and the discomfited husbands are thoroughly done for. A sprightly and taking play.

MICHAEL ERLE, THE MANIAC LOVER.

A romantic melodrama in 2 acts, by Thos. Egerton Wilks; 5 m. 3 f. Time, 1 h., 30 m. *Scenes:* Chamber and exteriors. This is a thrilling and touching play. It is very popular with amateurs. Michael Erle becomes insane because his sweetheart was taken from him by the wealthy Philip D'Arville. Years afterward Philip induces another young girl to meet him near the village church where a carriage is in waiting, and he carries her off, stabbing Michael, who attempts her rescue. On a subsequent occasion, the maniac returns to reason long enough to clear her good name. He stabs Philip, who, dying, rallies, and shoots Michael

ALL THAT GLITTERS IS NOT GOLD.

A comedy-drama in 2 acts, by Thos. and J.·M. Morton; 6 m , 3 f. Time, 2 h. *Scenes:* Handsome apartments. Jasper Plum is a wealthy cotton spinner. His son Stephen falls in love with Martha Gibbs, a factory girl. The elder Plum finally agrees that his son shall marry Martha if she will come and live in his house and bear herself with irreproachable demeanor for three months. Frederick Plum has married Valeria, the daughter of Lady Westendleigh. Valeria indiscreetly indulges in a flirtation, which, though proving innocent, was very dangerous. Martha, at the risk of her own reputation, saves her and is on the point of being driven in shame from the house when Valeria nobly confesses all. The closing scenes are very touching. This is a beautiful drama, well worthy the efforts of the best clubs

SLASHER AND CRASHER.

A farce, by John Madison Morton; 5 m., 2 f. Time, 50 m. *Scene:* A well furnished room. This play cannot be adequately described, but must be seen to be appreciated. Old Blowhard's fierce desire to have brave men for a son-in-law, and brother-in-law, and the abject cowardice of Sampson Slasher and Christopher Crasher, who aspire to those positions, furnish the pivot of the plot. Slasher and Crasher agree to work up a mock duel before Blowhard and Lieutenant Brown. It goes so far beyond Slasher's intentions that he falls into a perfect terror, whereat Crasher waxes still more brave. This scene is one of the most ludicrous imaginable, and never fails to set the audience roaring.

HAMLET.

By William Shakespeare. As arranged for the stage by Wilson Barrett; 12 m., 3 f., (lords, ladies etc.) Time, 3 h.

"Mr. Barrett has here presented the play in the most perfect form that it has ever been acted on the stage."   THE STAGE, London, October, 1884.

This edition is printed on good paper, with large clear type, and is suitable alike for the student, the teacher, the reader, the actor.

SUNDAY SCHOOL PIECES.

By PROF. J. H. GILMORE.

One Hundred and Eighteen Choice Pieces.

PRICE,   - - - -   25 CENTS.

PART ONE Embraces short poems for boys, girls and youths. All kinds of sentiment are included, from sacred poetry to that containing a humorous tinge.

PART TWO Includes prose declamations for boys, for girls, for young ladies, for young gentlemen, and *special* addresses, such as welcome to a pastor, address to the superintendent, to a visiting school, on the death of a teacher, presentation speeches, etc. These may be modified to suit *any* occasion in day school or elsewhere.

PART THREE Consists of dialogues for boys and girls, for boys alone, for girls alone, etc. ☞ *Most of this book is good for public school use.*

A NEW PLAY. (Alta Series.)

UNCLE JOSH.

A powerful farce-comedy in four acts, by Charles Townsend; 8 m , 3 f. Time, 2 h. 15 min. *Scenes:* parlor, apartments, street, saloon. *Characters:* Joshua Jarvis, from way down in Varmount, a capital old rustic of the Josh Whitcomb style; De Courville, (French) is a "heavy" villain of the best kind; Joe, his pal, is a bar-room tough and bunko steerer; Erastus, colored, is a screamer, and his experience with Upson Downes, the dude, will convulse the audience; Mulcahey, (Irish) is a typical saloon keeper; Minerva is an old maid willing to marry; Letty, a charming young lady the object of De Courville's wiles.

This play has a fine plot, thrilling situations, telling humor and everything needed to make it go. Not difficult to produce. (*Ready Nov. 1st,* 1891.)

PRICE,   : - - -   25 CENTS.

THE ETHIOPIAN DRAMA.

Price 15 Cents Each, Postpaid.

These plays are all short, and very funny. They serve admirably to give variety to a programme. The female characters may be assumed by males in most cases. Where something thoroughly comical is wanted, they are just the thing. Little or no stage apparatus is required. The number of darkies is given in those plays in which white characters occur.

STAGE STRUCK DARKY.

A very funny burlesque on high acting; 2 m., 1 f. Time, 10 m. Three negroes play Claude Melnotte, Lady Macbeth, Macduff, "Lucimicus," Damon and Pythias, etc.

STOCKS UP, STOCKS DOWN.

2 m. A played-out author and his sympathizing friend. Time, 8 m. Very funny, and full of business. Ludicrous description of a fire.

DEAF—IN A HORN.

2 m. Negro musician and a deaf pupil. Time, 8 m. The "pupil" has a large horn which he uses for an ear trumpet, pretending to be very deaf. By stratagem the teacher causes him to hear suddenly; comical business with the music, etc.

HANDY ANDY.

2 m., master and servant. Time, 12 m. The old man is petulant; the servant makes all sorts of ludicrous mistakes, and misunderstands every order. Very lively in action.

THE MISCHIEVOUS NIGGER.

A very popular negro farce; 4 m., 2 f. Time, 20 m. (Only one darky, the mischievous nigger.) *Scene*: Chamber with bedroom off. Requires two sham babies. *Characters*: Antony Snow (the nigger), old man, French barber, Irishman, nurse, Mrs. Norton.

THE SHAM DOCTOR.

A negro farce; 4 m., 2 f. Time, 15 m. Liverheel, a wood sawyer, turns doctor, and practices on "old Johnson," a colored brother. The sham doctor will bring down the house.

NO CURE, NO PAY.

3 m. (1 darky), 1 f. Time, 10 m. Will suit the most fastidious; a good piece for schools or parlor. Dr. Ipecac has a theory that excessive terror will cure the deaf and dumb. His daughter's lover is mistaken for the patient, to his infinite terror.

TRICKS.

A negro farce; 5 m., 2 f. Time, 10 m. (Only 2 darkies. 1 m., 1 f.) Mr. Growler determines to marry his ward for her money. Harry, her lover, lays a plan for elopement. The old man discovers it, and determines to be on hand himself. They in turn discover his plan, and send him off with the colored girl in disguise.

HAUNTED HOUSE.

2 m., landlord and a whitewasher (also 2 or 3 ghosts.) Time, 8 m. The whitewasher discovers spirits in a house where he is at work, and is frightened badly in consequence.

THE TWO POMPEYS.

4 m. Time. 8 m. A challenge to a duel is worked up in a very humorous manner until the courage oozes out of the duellists

AN UNHAPPY PAIR.

3 m. (and males for a band.) Time, 10 m. Two hungry "niggers" strike the musicians for a square meal. Good for school or parlor. Very funny; ends with a burlesque duet.

THE JOKE ON SQUINIM.

A negro farce (Black Statue improved), by W. B. Sheddaw; 4 m., 2 f. Time, 25 m. *Scenes*: A barn and a plain room. Mr. Squinim discovers his man, Pete, making love to Betsy, his daughter. He discharges Pete; the latter, with the assistance of Jake and a white man, is sold to Mr. Squinim as a statue (draped in a sheet), capable of imitating the movements of life. Jake takes the place of the statue, and when Mr. S. turns the crank, knocks him down, etc. No end of fun.

QUARRELSOME SERVANTS.

3 m. Time, 8 m. Mr. Jenkins is unable to procure servants who will not quarrel. He advertises for a male cook and a hostler. The interview with the candidates is uproariously comical. When Bill brings Mr. J.'s breakfast the fun becomes decidedly rich.

SPORTS ON A LARK.

3 m. Time, 8 m. Two niggers who are dead broke meet and get acquainted. B..gene St. Clair, who is out gunning, comes along. He has found a pocketbook, which they claim without success. They get his gun by chance and compel him to give up the pocketbook. By stratagem he recovers the gun. *Business* very lively and taking.

OTHELLO AND DESDEMONA.

2 m. Time, 12 m. A side splitting burlesque on the chamber scene in Othello. The strangling of "Desdemona" will bring down the house every time.

BACK FROM CALIFORNY; Or, Old Clothes.

3 m. Time, 12 m. Dr. Squozzle and Zip Johnson, a returned Californian, try to get some sleep in the office of a hotel while waiting for a train. Taking off their coats, etc., things get badly mixed and the clothes are locked in the wrong trunks. In the row that ensues Zip and Squozzle find they are brothers-in-law.

UNCLE JEFF.

A farce. 5 m. (2 negroes), 2 f. Time, 25 m. Uncle Jeff is full of mischief. Dr. Cole is in love with Mrs. Grimes. Harry, his son, is devoted to her daughter Josephine. The old folks oppose the match, and Uncle Jeff plays some queer jokes to assist Harry. A very popular farce.

ALL EXPENSES; Or, Nobody's Son.

2 m. Time 10 m. Artemus Buz is a manager, and Jemius Fluticus applies for a situation in his company. Very funny.

PROF. BLACK'S FUNNYGRAPH.

A nigger burlesque on the phonograph; 6 m., and niggers for audience (on the stage.) Time, 15 m. Prof. Black delivers to an appreciative audience a lecture on the wonderful funny-graph. The whole performance is as innocent as a spring lamb, and full of business as a spring goat.

JUMBO JUM.

A farce; 4 m (1 negro), 3 f. Time, 30 min. *Scenes:* Plain rooms and a garden. This is a popular farce wherever negro humor of the stage type is appreciated. Jumbo Jum is employed as a farm hand by Mr. Gobbleton. He proves to be a genuine African monkey who gets everything wrong end first in a most ludicrous way. The business is very lively and taking.

NEW PLAYS.

PRICE, - - - - - - - **FIFTEEN CENTS EACH.**

SEA DRIFT.

A stirring drama in 4 acts, by Harry Houston; 6 m., 2 f. (sailors, etc.) Time, about 2 hours. *Scenes:* The seacoast, cabin, gentleman's manor, landscape Storm scenes and very effective accessories. Within the capacity of any good club. Old Cripps and Monk are fine serio-tragic characters. Matt, called "Sea Drift," is a fine young-lady character of the uncut gem variety. Mother Carew, the crazy witch, is finely emotional. O'Dowd is a good typical Irishman, and Vesey a capital English dude. The perils of the orphan girl, Sea Drift, enlist at once the sympathies of the audience.

THE WEDDING TRIP.

A capital comedy in two acts, from the German of Benedix, by H. B. Sonneborn; 3 m., 2 f. Time, one hour. Drissler is a dry-as-dust professor in Kikeka College. He marries Cleopatra, a handsome young woman. He expects her to eat off a pine table and live as he had done while a bachelor. She decidedly objects, and the way she carries her point is thoroughly enjoyable. Digby and Delia, the servants, are capital comedy, and the professor is a capital "freak." Sure to take.

BLIND MARGARET.

A musical sketch, from Longfellow's poem of the same name, by Caroline E. Thompson; 3 m., 3 f., and chorus. Time, 30 minutes. Original music for the refrain.

THE WOMAN HATER.

A farce from the German of Benedix, by Hilton B. Sonneborn; 2 m., 1 f. Time, 30 minutes Betsey and Gus are newly married, and G is inclined to be jealous of his bride. Frelin, a friend of Gus, has been jilted, and becomes a woman hater. He visits Gus and B., and acts like a bear at first. Betsey, by an innocent stratagem, contrives to make him admit the charms of the fair sex; at the same time she wins a philopena from her jealous husband. Excellent.

WHO TOLD THE LIE?

Farce from the German, by H. B. Sonneborn; 5 m., 3 f. Time, 30 minutes. The plot hinge on the concealment by Edith Stevens, an heiress, of some men suspected of engaging in a street riot. She invites them to tea, and furnishes them with disguises. For a time they cleverly elude the police and her guardian. One of the suspects turns out to be an old lover. Good German and Irish Characters

AMATEURS' SUPPLIES.

TABLEAU LIGHTS.—A tableau has usually little effect unless strongly illuminated. Several colors, but *red*, *green* and *white*, answer nearly all purposes.

Place in a dish or on a brick, and ignite with a match. Persons often ask, Do these lights produce disagreeable fumes? All chemical lights produce *some* smoke and odor.

Price per package (for two Tableaux)... $ .50

" per pound (assorted colors)............ .... 1.75

Packages double size, and sufficient for the *Second Illumination.*

MAGNESIUM LIGHT.—A metal ribbon which may be ignited with a common match....

Brilliant, whitish light. Every one should see this beautiful light, *entirely free* from smoke or odor. Price by mail, postpaid .... .25

BURNT CORK, per Box... .30

LIGHTNING, per Box........ 40

SPIRIT GUM, per Bottle (not mailable)... .25

BLUE for Unshaven Faces in Comedy Characters, per Box......................... .25

CARMINE, to heighten effect of Burnt Cork, per Box............................ .30

DUTCH PINK, for Sallow Complexions, per Box................................... .25

JOINING PASTE, for joining Wigs to Forehead, per Stick........................ .25

MONGOLIAN, for Indians, Mulattoes, etc., per Box.............................. .30

RUDDY ROUGE, for Low Comedy, Seamen, etc., per Box............................ .30

WHITING, for Pantomimes, Clowns, Statuary, etc., per Box...... .... .25

CHROME, for sallow complexions, lightening eyebrows, mustaches, etc.......... .25

PREPARED FULLER'S EARTH, to powder face before making up .... .30

MAKE UP PENCILS, Light Flesh, Dark Flesh, Brown, Black, White, Gray, Carmine,

Blue and Lake, per Set.. $1.00

LINING PENCILS, each.. .25

HELMER'S MAKE UP BOOK, tells how to make up and use all articles needed by

Amateurs. An invaluable assistant....... .... .25

WHISKERS AND MUSTACHES.

Side Whiskers and Mustache on Gauze.... ... . $2.00

Side Whiskers and Mustache on Wire... 1.50

Side Whiskers without Mustache on Gauze.. 1.50

Side Whiskers without Mustache on Wire... 1.00

Full Beard 1.50

Full Beard without Mustache.. 1.25

Mustache with Chin Beard combined.. 2.00

Chin Beard... 1.25

Imperial (with wax).. .30

Mustache (with wax) on Gauze... .35

WIGS.

Negro... Black, $1.25; Gray, $2.00

Clown, in Colors... 4.50

Clown, Bald.. 2.00

Irish (crop)... 4.50

Bald... 4.50

Ordinary Dress (all colors)............. .... 4.50

Fancy Dress.. $6.00 to 10.00

CRAPE HAIR, different colors, for making mustaches, etc., per yard.............. .25

☞ In ordering Wigs give Size of Hat. State Color wanted on all Hair Goods.

Hair goods mailed free; I do not keep Wigs in stock, but get them made to order. Usually goods can be sent by return mail or express, but it is best to allow a margin of two or three days.

C. O. D. orders *must* be accompanied by twenty per cent. of price of goods. Do not send orders by telegraph on a few hours' notice.

☞ I can furnish any article needed by Amateurs.

T. S. DENISON, Publisher,

163 Randolph Street, CHICAGO.

AMATEURS' SUPPLIES.

Bole Armenia, in Sunburnt Characters........ .... 20c.
Face Powders, White, Pink, Brunette............................ 25c.
Eye Brow Pencils, Blue, Black, Brown........................... 25c.
Email Noir, Black, for stopping out Teeth.......................... 20c.
Theater Rouge.. .... 25c.
Hair Powders, White, Gold, Silver, Diamond, Bronze and Blonde, each. 25c.
Powder Puffs..10c. to 50c.
Grenadine Rouge, for the Lips........................... 25c.
Hares' Feet .... 25c.
"   "   Ivory handle. .... 50c.
India Ink... 10c.
Stomps, Leather (for lining)..................................... 20c.
"   Paper.. .... 05c.
Nose Putty, for Building up the Nose.......................... 25c.
Cocoa Butter, for removing Grease Paint..................... 25c.
Vaseline, for removing Grease Paint.................... ..... 25c.
Curling Irons, all sizes, from......................10c. to $1.50

GREASE PAINTS.

No. 1. Very Pale Flesh Color.	No. 10. Sallow, for Old Age.
" 2. Light Flesh, Deeper Tint.	" 11. Ruddy, " "
" 3. Natural Flesh Color for Juvenile Heroes.	" 12. Olive, Healthy.
" 4. Rose Tint " " "	" 13. " Lighter Shade.
" 5. Deeper Shade " " "	" 14. Gipsey Flesh Color.
" 6. Healthy Sunburnt " "	" 15. Othello.
" 7. " " Deeper Shade.	" 16. Chinese.
" 8. Sallow, for Young Men.	" 17. Indian.
" 9. Healthy Color, for Middle Ages.	" 18. East Indian.

(Done up in Sticks of 8 inches in length at 50c. each.)

MAKE UP BOX, Contains

A Set of Grease Paints, light and dark flesh, brown, black, white, blue, gray, light and dark rouge—Powder Puff—Cocoa Butter—2 Brushes—1 Theater Rouge —Grenadine—Spirit Gum—India Ink—Mirror—Hare's Foot—2 Stomps—2 Shades Water Cosmetique—Cosmetique Brush—2 Shades Face Powder—Email Noir— Scissors—Crape Hair—Nose Putty and Mustache Cosmetique. $5.00.

MISS BEACH'S CURLING FLUID

Keeps the hair in curl for days. **No Odor or Sediment. Harmless.** Gives vigor and beauty to hair, increases its growth. **A Toilet Necessity. During rehearsals and at parties or other public assemblies, ladies have great difficulty in keeping their hair neat with the appearance of natural curls. This preparation is all that is claimed for it. Give it a trial. At druggists or sent prepaid, 50c. Lady Agents wanted.**

T. S. DENISON,

163 Randolph Street,   -   -   -   CHICAGO, ILL.